"Your timing is perfect," Jared said, reaching for the baby bottle she'd brought.

When her fingers brushed his, it was all Faith could do to ignore the faint tremor of awareness that shimmied up her arm.

"He slept longer than I thought he would," Faith commented as Jared walked to the rocking chair and sat down.

Mesmerized, Faith lingered near the door, watching Jared settle Nicky into a comfortable position against his chest.

"You don't have to stay and supervise," Jared told her in a low voice. "I assure you I'm quite capable of feeding and burping my son."

Faith met his gaze. "I wasn't—"

"Or are you hanging around for another reason?" he asked, his gaze drifting over her scanty attire.

Her breath caught in her throat at the blatant sexual undertone in his voice. He thought she was her identical twin—the mother of his child!

Dear Reader,

As spring turns to summer, make Silhouette Romance the perfect companion for those lazy days and sultry nights! Fans of our LOVING THE BOSS series won't want to miss *The Marriage Merger* by exciting author Vivian Leiber. A pretend engagement between friends goes awry when their white lies lead to a *real* white wedding!

Take one biological-clock-ticking twin posing as a new mom and one daddy determined to gain custody of his newborn son, and you've got the unsuspecting partners in *The Baby Arrangement,* Moyra Tarling's tender BUNDLES OF JOY title. You've asked for more TWINS ON THE DOORSTEP, Stella Bagwell's charming author-led miniseries, so this month we give you *Millionaire on Her Doorstep,* an emotional story of two wounded souls who find love in the most unexpected way...and in the most unexpected place.

Can a bachelor bent on never marrying and a single mom with a bustling brood of four become a *Fairy-Tale Family?* Find out in Pat Montana's delightful new novel. Next, a handsome doctor's case of mistaken identity leads to *The Triplet's Wedding Wish* in this heartwarming tale by DeAnna Talcott. And a young widow finds the home—and family—she's always wanted when she strikes a deal with a *Nevada Cowboy Dad,* this month's FAMILY MATTERS offering from Dorsey Kelley.

Enjoy this month's fantastic selections, and make sure to return each and every month to Silhouette Romance!

Mary-Theresa Hussey

Mary-Theresa Hussey
Senior Editor, Silhouette Romance

Please address questions and book requests to:
Silhouette Reader Service
U.S.: 3010 Walden Ave., P.O. Box 1325, Buffalo, NY 14269
Canadian: P.O. Box 609, Fort Erie, Ont. L2A 5X3

THE BABY ARRANGEMENT

Moyra Tarling

Silhouette

ROMANCE™

Published by Silhouette Books

America's Publisher of Contemporary Romance

For new mothers and fathers everywhere.
Enjoy every minute, because they'll be all grown
before you know it!

 SILHOUETTE BOOKS

ISBN 0-373-19367-X

THE BABY ARRANGEMENT

Copyright © 1999 by Moyra Tarling

Look us up on-line at: http://www.romance.net

Printed in U.S.A.

MOYRA TARLING

was born in Aberdeenshire, Scotland. It was there that she was first introduced to, and became hooked on, romance novels. In 1968, she immigrated to Vancouver, Canada, where she met and married her husband. They have two grown children. Empty nesters now, they enjoy taking trips in their getaway van and browsing in antique shops for corkscrews and buttonhooks. But Moyra's favorite pastime is curling up with a great book—a romance, of course! Moyra loves to hear from readers. You can write to her at P.O. Box 161, Blaine, WA 98231-D161.

Dear Reader,

Babies are indeed BUNDLES OF JOY, precious
gifts to be loved, cherished and protected. In
The Baby Arrangement Nicky is just such a baby. I
knew when Faith saw her tiny, innocent and beautiful
nephew, she would feel the same overwhelming love
and need to protect that I felt when my newborn son
was first placed in my arms.

It is heartwarming to know that most fathers, upon
seeing their child for the first time, feel the exact same
sense of wonder, the same deep love as well as a fierce
need to protect.

Jared is that kind of man, that kind of hero. By bringing
him and Faith together, I knew these two caring, loving
people, committed to doing what was best for Nicky,
deserved to fall in love. Deserved to become the family
they both longed for.

I hope you enjoy reading *The Baby Arrangement* as
much as I enjoyed writing it.

Much love,

Moyra Tarling

Chapter One

He was too late. He'd been knocking on the door of the house for at least ten minutes, to no avail. He'd missed her. She'd vanished for a second time, taking his infant son with her.

Jared McAndrew cursed as he climbed into his car. He slammed his hands against the steering wheel as the familiar feelings of frustration and anger churned to life within him.

He'd come close...so close. Silently he vowed not to quit until he'd tracked down his newborn son, a son he'd never seen.

Muttering under his breath, Jared reached for the key to restart the engine.

It was at that precise moment he spotted the baby stroller as it turned into the leaf-covered driveway. His heart shuddered to a halt, and he felt his breath back up in his throat as he focused his gaze on the mother of his child.

He blinked several times, fearful his eyes were playing tricks on him. But there was no mistake. Reaching for the door handle, Jared was out of the car in a flash.

Faith Nelson slowed the baby stroller to a halt the minute she saw the sleek black car parked in her driveway. She watched as a tall, dark-haired man dressed in crumpled gray slacks and a navy sweater emerged from the front seat.

Her heart slammed against her ribs and a ripple of apprehension chased down her spine at the look of fury she could see etched on the stranger's handsome features. Instinctively she tightened her fingers on the handle of the baby stroller as his long strides ate up the driveway.

"Hello, Paula," the man said, coming to a halt a few feet in front of the stroller. "You look surprised to see me." His voice was deep and resonant, but with an edge that could easily have cut glass.

Faith moistened lips that were suddenly dry. "I'm sorry. I'm not—"

"You're sorry!" the man interrupted, his voice quavering with barely suppressed rage.

"You don't understand," Faith said, but before she could even begin to explain, his eyes flashed with a look of contempt that effectively silenced her.

"Oh…you've got that right," he drawled. "But then I doubt I'll ever understand how you could disappear without a word," he said. "We had an agreement, remember? Did you really think I wouldn't come looking for you?''

At his challenging tone an icy rivulet slithered down Faith's back, and she cast a quick glance toward the house.

''Don't even think about it,'' the man said, taking a step closer. ''I've come for my son. I'm taking him home with me, and I'd advise you not to try to stop me,'' he added, and dropped into a crouched position in front of the stroller.

''But you can't...'' Faith protested, looking around in the hope a police car might happen to be cruising the area.

''Just watch me,'' he replied.

''Please, you don't understand. I'm not...'' Faith tried anew to explain, but the words dissolved in her throat when she saw the harsh angry lines on his face vanish, replaced by an expression of awe.

''He's beautiful....'' The words were a mere whisper of sound as Jared stared in wonderment at the tiny but perfect infant asleep in the stroller. Not even seeing the grainy pictures of his unborn son on the hospital sonogram had prepared him for this heart-stopping moment.

Gazing for the very first time at his own flesh and blood, his own son, an avalanche of emotions more powerful than anything he'd ever felt before gripped him, squeezing his heart and bringing tears to his eyes.

The intensity of his feelings caught him completely off guard, and so too did the sudden and urgent need to make sure he wasn't dreaming. Reaching out, he gently touched his son's smooth cheek.

At the contact Jared felt a tightening in his chest. As his glance drifted over the baby's angelic face, he noted with some pride the shock of jet black hair peeking out from beneath a knitted blue bonnet.

Inhaling deeply, he caught the sweet scent of baby powder mixed with milky formula. He silently acknowledged that nothing in his thirty-seven years had prepared him for such a profound moment.

Jared released the breath he hadn't realized he was holding. As he withdrew his hand he made a promise to his son, to be a loving, caring father—the kind of father he himself had longed for as a child.

Faith watched the array of emotions flitting across the stranger's face and felt as if her heart were being torn from her body. Stifling a moan, she began to push the stroller toward the house.

"Hey! Just a minute." Jared stretched to his full height and came marching after her. He grabbed the handle of the stroller, halting her progress. "You're not running out on me again."

He watched as tears pooled in her eyes.

"And you can cut the tearful act, Paula," Jared continued, his tone scathing. "After what you've put me through these past two weeks, I'm not going to fall for that old trick. I'm here for one reason, and one reason only—to take my son home."

Faith bravely met his fierce glare. That the

stranger had mistaken her for her identical twin sister, Paula, was obvious, and from the description Paula had given her, he in turn could only be Jared McAndrew, the baby's father. But why hadn't Paula bothered to mention she'd been running away from the man?

"If you'd just let me finish…" Faith tried again, but this time her attempts to explain were suddenly drowned out by a baby's cry.

Startled, they both stared at the source of the sound. The volume of the cries increased, and Faith quickly took control. Bending, she lifted the infant into her arms, hugging him to her. Rocking him gently, she crooned words of comfort.

Over the baby's shoulder she met the stranger's piercing gaze, daring him to challenge her. But when she glimpsed the anxiety shimmering in the depths of his blue eyes, her heart contracted.

"He's hungry," she told him. "And he doesn't like to be kept waiting," she added, moving past him toward the front door.

Faith dug in to her jacket pocket and located her keys. Opening the door, she threw a quick glance over her shoulder. It came as no surprise to see Jared McAndrew following her, bringing the baby stroller with him.

Once inside, Faith headed for the kitchen. Earlier that morning, before Nicky had awakened, she'd made up several bottles for him. Retrieving one from the fridge, she crossed to the sink.

"You're not breast-feeding. Good. That will simplify matters," the baby's father said, standing in the doorway.

Faith fought down the bubble of hysterical laughter threatening to break free. "No, I'm not breast-feeding," she responded, filling the bowl in the sink with hot water from the tap. Dropping the baby's bottle into it, she turned to face the man hovering behind her like a vulture.

"He needs to be changed, then fed," Faith said assertively. "When I'm finished feeding him, we'll get this sorted out."

"I'm not going anywhere," he replied. "Besides, what's there to sort out? I thought I'd made myself perfectly clear. Once you've finished feeding my son, I'm taking him home with me."

A variety of emotions ranging from fear to frustration tugged at Faith, but she kept them in check. This wasn't the time to argue, not when she had a hungry baby in her arms.

She strode down the hall and into her bedroom. After Paula had left for the airport last night, Faith had transported her dressing table into a makeshift change table by placing a thick bath towel on top of it.

Not for the first time since her twin had appeared on her doorstep twelve hours ago, Faith wondered what kind of mess her sister had gotten herself into.

Precocious and outgoing as a youngster, Paula had been the favorite child. Their parents had indulged her and encouraged her in her goal to become an actress. Faith, shyer and more introverted, had sat in the shadows, quietly developing her artistic talent, a talent that had led her to a career illustrating children's books.

Throughout their teenage years Paula had landed herself in more scrapes than Faith cared to recall. She'd delighted in pulling reckless and sometimes dangerous stunts with no thought to the consequences.

Faith, a scant ten minutes older than her twin, had often been left to soothe ruffled feathers, pacify angry neighbors, or take the blame for things her sister had done.

After graduating from high school, Paula had moved to Los Angeles, where she'd worked as a waitress before landing a small part in a movie. From there she'd moved to New York to work in an off-Broadway show.

Faith in turn had won a scholarship to attend an artists' college in Seattle. Living on opposite sides of the country, they'd drifted apart. Paula hadn't been able to attend Faith's small wedding. The last time Faith had seen her twin had been almost two years ago, at Erica's funeral. After a brief stay Paula had returned to the East Coast, still chasing her dream of stardom.

But while Paula's arrival yesterday had surprised her, it was nothing compared to the shock of having her twin thrust a baby into her arms and beg for her help. At the time, Faith had wondered if by some quirk of fate she'd stepped into a nightmare.

Suddenly Nicky's cries grew more urgent, effectively bringing her thoughts back to the present. With quick, accomplished movements she changed his diaper all the while speaking softly to him till his cries subsided. As she gazed down at his cherublike face she noticed for the first time the faint cleft in his chin—a tiny replica of his father's.

Snapping the sleeper back into place, Faith lifted Nicky from the dresser, carefully supporting his neck and head. The powdery scent of baby wrapped around her, filling her senses and storming her defenses. Suddenly a barrage of memories, memories of another baby—her daughter, Erica—washed over her. Erica had been born prematurely with a multitude of medical problems, problems that after only five days had resulted in her death.

Faith bit down on the inner softness of her mouth to stop the moan of pain and sadness threatening to escape. Blinking back tears, she firmly closed the door on the past, a past too painful to revisit.

Turning, she came to an abrupt halt when she found Jared McAndrew's tall frame blocking the doorway.

"Excuse me," she said, careful to avoid his gaze, unwilling to let him see her distress.

"I'm impressed, Paula," he said moving aside. "You looked like you knew what you were doing. Did you take a crash course in child care?" he asked, cynicism in his voice.

Faith made no reply as she headed for the kitchen.

"So tell me, who owns the house?" Jared asked

as he followed her down the hall. "Is it one of your actor friends…or an old lover, perhaps?"

Faith ignored him. Grabbing a tea towel off the counter, she retrieved the bottle of formula from the sink. Continuing into the tiny living room, she sat down in front of the bay window in the rocking chair she'd bought during her own pregnancy.

With practiced ease she tested the temperature of the milk on the inside of her wrist. Nicky was growing increasingly fretful, squirming in earnest now, undoubtedly aware nourishment was close at hand. Faith nestled the baby firmly against her breast, and in a matter of seconds his eager mouth found the bottle's nipple.

Closing her eyes, Faith drew a steadying breath. As she gently rocked back and forth she listened to the soft sucking sound Nicky made, a noise she'd never thought to hear again, and one that made her heart ache anew.

After a few moments Faith ventured to open her eyes. The baby's father had followed her into the living room and was slumped in the big old armchair opposite, eyes closed and a look of exhaustion on his face.

She let her gaze travel over his arresting features; the wide intelligent forehead, the straight nose, the mouth that was full and sensual, hair as black as ebony and the attractive cleft in his chin that Paula had mentioned.

Dropping her gaze to the sleeping child once more, Faith let her thoughts drift back to the events

of the previous night. Why hadn't Paula warned her
to expect the baby's father?

"I've made such a mess of things," Paula had
said, carrying the stroller and diaper bag inside. "I
didn't know where else to go."

Faith had swallowed the hard lump of emotion
clogging her throat. "The baby's yours?" She'd felt
foolish posing the question, but she hadn't even
known her twin was pregnant.

"Yes, he's mine," Paula had confirmed with a
heavy sigh, and Faith had heard neither pride nor
joy in her sister's voice. "It wasn't supposed to happen," her twin had continued, annoyance echoing
in every word. "I forgot to take a few pills...that's
all."

"That's all," Faith repeated, and lifted her gaze
to meet Paula's, wondering if her sister ever thought
about the consequences of her actions.

"You're not going to start lecturing me or anything, are you?"

"No, I'm not going to lecture you," Faith assured
her, suddenly blinking away the moisture clinging
to her lashes. "Mom and Dad must be thrilled..."
she went on, and immediately caught the look of
guilt that flashed in her sister's eyes.

"Haven't you told them?" Faith asked as she followed Paula into the living room.

"No, I haven't told them," Paula confessed.
Dropping into the armchair, she glanced up at Faith.
"I haven't told anybody. I couldn't—" She stopped

abruptly. "Not after what you went through with Erica," she added, her voice trailing off.

"I see," Faith responded softly, surprised and touched by her sister's thoughtfulness.

Glancing at her twin, Faith noted the paleness of her sister's features, as well as the anxiety tugging at her mouth.

"So, tell me. What kind of mess have you gotten yourself into this time?" Faith asked as she lowered herself with the baby into the love seat facing the granite fireplace.

"It's complicated..." Paula replied, not quite meeting Faith's eyes.

"When hasn't your life been complicated? You thrive on complicated," she added in an attempt to coax a smile from her twin.

Paula flashed her a fleeting grin. "I know. But this time, well...this time I think I've bitten off more than I can chew," she concluded with a sigh.

Faith remained silent, knowing from experience it was futile to ask questions. Paula, if she felt so inclined, would explain in her own sweet time.

"How old is the baby?" Faith asked as the subject of her question began to wriggle in her arms. "And if I'm not out of line...who's the father? Anyone I know?"

"The baby was born September fifteenth."

"That's just two weeks ago. And the father?" she prompted.

Paula leaned back in the armchair. "His name's Jared McAndrew. He's not an actor, if that's what you're thinking," she added. "Well, his mother was an actress, but that doesn't count."

"Not an actor... Now, there's a twist," Faith commented dryly.

Paula's grin appeared again. "He's a lawyer, if you must know."

"A lawyer!" Faith pretended to be shocked. "How on earth did you get involved with a lawyer?"

"I met him through a mutual friend. At first I thought he was an actor. He's certainly handsome enough, with gorgeous blue eyes, dark brooding looks and a cleft in his chin that's very sexy." She lapsed into silence, a small smile tugging at her mouth.

Faith waited for her twin to say more, but she appeared to be deep in thought. "Has the baby got a name?" Faith finally asked.

"Yes. His name is Nicholas Preston McAndrew. I named him after Grandpa Preston," Paula answered, her tone softening a little with sentimentality as she spoke of their own beloved grandfather. "He's much too little to be called Nicholas, so I just call him Nicky."

"Grandpa would have been proud and pleased," Faith replied, still finding it difficult to come to terms with the fact that the baby in her arms actually belonged to her sister. Marriage and children had always been high on Faith's list of goals, but nowhere on Paula's.

"Does the nonactor, not-in-show-business lawyer know he's a father?"

"Yes. Jared knows," Paula responded. "Listen, sis, I'm a wreck and too exhausted to think, let alone explain everything. What I need is a couple of hours uninterrupted shut-eye. This mothering routine has worn me out. I'm beginning to think I'm not cut out for it. I haven't had a decent night's sleep since before he was born."

Faith hid a smile. "Welcome to the real world," she said. "Go take a nap. The bed in the spare room is always made up."

"Thanks." Paula rose from the armchair. She'd taken only a couple of steps when she stopped and turned to Faith. "Uh...it is all right. I mean, you don't mind looking after the baby, do you?" she asked with some hesitation.

Faith lifted her gaze from the sleeping infant and smiled at her twin. "No, I don't mind," she answered, surprised and pleased to discover she was speaking the truth.

She hadn't as much as looked at a baby, never mind held one, since Erica's death. In fact, Faith had deliberately made a point of avoiding situations where she might run into anyone with an infant.

But feeling the weight of Nicky in her arms, mingled with his sweet scent, was strangely comforting. Watching his chest rise and fall, she was mesmerized by the miracle in her arms. And holding him seemed to diminish the pain of her loss and restore a small measure of peace.

"Well, Nicky," Faith said softly, once Paula had disappeared down the hallway. "I guess it's just you and me. By the way, I'm your aunt Faith." Nicky's eyes flickered open in response to her voice, and seconds later he started to cry.

Carrying him into her bedroom, Faith proceeded to change and feed the infant. Afterward, she put him down in the center of her king-size bed for a nap while she tidied her workroom. Just that morning a courier had picked up the children's illustrations she'd completed for her publisher.

Paula joined her in the kitchen two hours later. After inquiring about Nicky, she filled a glass with orange juice and turned to Faith. "Listen, sis, I have to fly to L.A. tonight," Paula suddenly announced.

"Tonight?" Faith repeated with a frown. "But you just got here," she added, disappointment tugging at her because Paula and the baby had to leave so soon.

"It's really important," Paula continued. "It could be the turning point of my career. That's why I had to—" She broke off. "I need to get there as soon as I can. I've waited so long for this and I can't afford to blow it...."

"Blow what?" Faith asked, but Paula merely shook her head and brought the glass to her lips.

Paula sighed. "I don't have time to explain all the ins and outs. I have to catch a plane. But I need to ask a favor," she hurried on.

"Anything. You know that," Faith responded,

wondering if Paula would ever tell her the whole story.

"Can I leave Nicky with you?" Paula asked.

Startled, Faith felt her breath catch in her throat at the unexpected request.

"I know it's asking a lot...."

"What about his father? Can't you leave Nicky with him?"

Paula hesitated, and avoided Faith's gaze. "Right now, that's not an option. And please don't ask me why," Paula hurried on. "Look, it'll only be for a couple of days...a week at the most."

Faith heard the familiar pleading note in her twin's voice. Reaching for the towel on the drain board, she dried her hands. "Of course I'll look after Nicky," she said. "Take as long as you need."

Paula's eyes instantly lit up, her features relaxing in obvious relief. "Do you mean it?" she asked breathlessly.

"When have I ever been able to say no to my baby sister?" Faith teased gently.

Faith suddenly found herself enfolded in Paula's arms. "Oh, sis, thanks. This means a lot to me," Paula mumbled before spinning away. "Oh...can I borrow some clothes? I was in such a hurry when I left, I didn't think to take any of my regular clothes with me. I'll hit the stores once I get to L.A."

"Sure. Check in my closet," Faith said, only just managing to refrain from voicing the question *Left where?* "There's not a lot to choose from, but help yourself," she added.

Paula had phoned the airline and, after making a reservation, had called for a taxi. While they'd waited for the cab Faith had tried to coax some more information from her twin, but Paula had ignored her questions, and had simply kept repeating that her future depended on the outcome of the trip.

"I'll know more when I get there," Paula had said when the cab finally arrived. "I'll call tomorrow morning, say around ten," she'd said, and, giving Faith a final hug, she'd climbed into the taxi.

But Paula hadn't called, at least not yet. Faith set the empty baby bottle on the end table beside her. She glanced at her watch. It was past nine-thirty. Shifting Nicky to her right shoulder, she began to rub his back in slow, circular motions.

Faith's gaze drifted to the man dozing in the armchair. There could be no mistake. The description Paula had given her of Jared McAndrew the night before fitted him to a T.

Asleep, he looked considerably less threatening. Several strands of jet black hair had fallen across his forehead, affording him a boyish, almost youthful appearance. But she only had to transfer her attention to the dark shadow outlining his jaw to dispel that notion.

Nonetheless, Jared McAndrew's threat to take Nicky was definitely real. A shiver chased down Faith's spine. Should she call the police? she wondered. But even if she did, could they do anything to prevent him from taking Nicky?

Paula hadn't left her the baby's birth certificate or any documentation to prove she was related to the child. And besides, Paula had said Jared was a lawyer, and in all likelihood that would work in his favor.

Why hadn't her twin warned her to be on the lookout for Nicky's father? What had happened between them? Suddenly Faith recalled the comments Jared had made outside earlier, implying Paula had been running away. But why?

It appeared he was unaware Paula had a twin sister, and Faith wondered if keeping that knowledge to herself, at least for time being, might give her a slight edge.

She glanced again at his sleeping figure. The idea of tiptoeing past him and making her escape with Nicky was very tempting, but she sensed if she tried to leave, he would awaken.

Deciding to test her theory, she tightened her hold on the baby and with her pulse starting to race, she carefully eased herself out of the rocking chair.

She'd barely taken a step before the stranger's dark, sweeping lashes lifted and a pair of piercing blue eyes met hers.

"Going somewhere?" He jerked upright into a sitting position.

"Nicky's asleep," Faith told him. "I was going to put him down for a nap."

"You named the baby Nicky?" Jared asked, rising from the chair to effectively bar her exit.

"Nicholas," she corrected, taking a step back.

"Nicholas McAndrew..." he said, testing out the name. He glanced at the sleeping child in her arms and a slow smile tugged at the corners of his mouth. "Nicholas McAndrew. I like it. It's got a nice ring to it."

"I'm glad you approve," Faith said, fighting to keep the sarcasm out of her voice.

"But there's no point putting the baby to bed," he told her evenly.

"Why not?" Faith took another step back, his nearness making her feel a little claustrophobic.

"Because I'm taking him home to Grace Harbor with me."

"Grace Harbor?" Faith repeated, never having heard of the place.

"Come on, Paula," he said, his tone scathing. "I don't know what game you're playing, but it cuts no ice with me. We had a deal, signed and sealed. And if you think you can back out of it now, you're very much mistaken."

"A deal? What deal?" Instinctively, Faith tightened her hold on the baby, making him squirm a little in his sleep.

She watched a shadow pass over Jared's handsome features at her words, and a look of anger darkened his eyes.

"Don't play the innocent with me. You know damned well what I'm talking about." His tone was icy as he held out his hands toward her. "If you'll give me my son, we'll get out of your life."

Faith stared in bewilderment at the man's outstretched hands. Regardless of the deal he'd referred to, a deal she had no knowledge of and one he'd made with Paula, Faith simply couldn't bring herself to hand Nicky over to him and let him walk out.

She'd made a promise to look after Nicky until Paula returned from L.A.... It was a promise she intended to keep.

"I can't do that," Faith stated with a calmness she was far from feeling. "Where Nicky goes, I go!" she blurted out, and had the satisfaction of seeing Jared McAndrew's blue eyes widen with surprise.

Chapter Two

Jared held Paula's gaze for several long seconds. Her announcement had caught him off guard, but what he found even more disturbing was the protective, almost possessive way she was holding on to the baby.

"Don't you have an audition to go to?" he asked. "I thought you were anxious to get back to L.A. and your career."

"Not at the moment," Faith responded, yet knowing her twin's trip to L.A. undoubtedly had everything to do with Paula wanting to resume her acting career. "Besides, how are you proposing to take care of Nicky while you drive? I didn't see a proper safety seat in your car. Maybe you were planning to toss Nicky into the back seat and let him fend for himself."

Jared bristled at her sarcastic tone. In his race to

reach San Francisco before she disappeared again, his only thought had been to find his son. He hadn't considered the need for a car seat to transport the baby home.

"And where would I find a car seat?" he asked.

"There's a baby store in the mall a couple of blocks away. You could drive there now," she suggested, pleased he appeared concerned with Nicky's safety.

"And while I'm driving around looking for a store that probably doesn't exist, you'll take Nicky and run," he countered in a cynical tone. "I don't think so. But nice try."

Faith shrugged her shoulders. She wasn't lying— the store she'd mentioned was located in a shopping mall only a few blocks away—but his mocking tone left her in no doubt he didn't trust her...or more accurately, he didn't trust Paula.

Somehow she'd have to stall for time, at least until Paula called...if she called. Faith bit back a sigh, wishing that Paula had told her more about the mess she was in, and about the angry, cynical and distrustful man who was Nicky's father.

"You're not serious about coming back to Grace Harbor, are you?" Jared's question startled her, and she met his gaze head-on.

"Of course I'm serious," she responded, anger edging her tone.

"I thought you couldn't wait to get out of there."

The baby shifted in her arms as if to remind them

both of his presence. "Nicky's only two weeks old. He needs me."

Faith saw the pulse throbbing at Jared's jaw, and knew by the tension emanating from him that he was fighting an internal battle. "How long will it take to get the baby ready?" he asked abruptly. "We have a long drive ahead."

Relief spiraled through her. "Half an hour, maybe more," she said, and without waiting for a reply she swept past him into the hallway.

Jared let out the breath trapped in his lungs. He didn't know what to make of Paula's behavior. She'd sounded sincere just now when she'd said the baby needed her.

It had to be an act! Giving birth couldn't possibly have brought about such a dramatic and profound transformation, awakening the maternal instincts she'd assured him she didn't possess.

A leopard couldn't change its spots. And if he'd learned anything about the woman during the five months she'd spent under his roof, it was that while she might have a conscience—why else had she gone through with the pregnancy instead of aborting the child?—her ultimate goal of becoming an actress remained unchanged.

Jared cursed under his breath. His thoughts drifted back to the first time he'd met Paula. He'd still been living in L.A. then, and they'd been seated next to each other at a dinner party given by one of Jared's clients. Beautiful and confident, she'd dazzled him with her smile. He'd admired her determination to succeed as an actress.

Though as a rule he avoided dating would-be starlets, he'd accepted her invitation about a week later to partner her to a party. They'd gone out several times after that, but lost touch once he moved to Grace Harbor.

But on a visit to L.A., he'd run into her at one of his old favorite haunts. She was celebrating her birthday with friends and insisted he join them. On impulse he'd invited her back to his hotel room for a nightcap. They'd had several, and later he wasn't sure who had seduced whom....

When she'd tracked him down to tell him she was carrying his child, he'd asked her to marry him.

She'd laughed and turned him down. He'd quickly realized she had an agenda all her own, an agenda that didn't include raising a child.

That's when the lawyer in him had taken over. He'd drawn up an agreement, one he believed was in the child's best interests, one stating she would give him full custody of the baby once it was born.

The reason he'd wanted to put everything in writing was to protect his son. That desire had stemmed from memories of his own childhood, a childhood spent being dragged around the country by his mother, a struggling actress, who'd been bent on chasing her own dream of stardom.

He'd grown to hate the life-style she'd subjected him to, the instability, the nomadic existence, and he'd been adamant no child of his would suffer as he had.

Paula had seemed relieved at his willingness to assume full responsibility for the child. She'd signed the papers without protest, assuring him acting was all she'd ever wanted to do, and that he needn't worry about her changing her mind. Under the terms of the agreement, Paula had moved in to the guest room at his home in Oregon to await the birth of the baby.

She'd stuck rigidly to the high-protein diet and regular exercise the doctor had recommended, succeeding in keeping her weight gain to a minimum. But that hadn't stopped her grumbling about her expanding waistline and complaining daily about how the pregnancy was ruining her figure.

She'd grown restless and impatient for the birth to be over, and as her due date drew near, Jared had awakened several times during the night to hear Paula talking on the phone. Everything had been going according to plan, and he'd convinced himself she was simply making arrangements for her return to L.A.

But two days before the baby's due date, she'd suddenly and inexplicably disappeared, leaving him shaken, confused and very angry.

After hiring a private detective to find her, he'd called every hospital in Oregon and Washington in an attempt to locate her himself, to no avail.

The only explanation he could think of for her

abrupt departure was she'd had a change of heart…and had decided to keep the baby after all.

While he longed to reject the notion out of hand, he found he couldn't dismiss it altogether, not after watching the loving way she'd changed and fed the baby. Nor could he quite forget the hint of sadness he'd glimpsed in the shimmering depths of her green eyes…a sadness that puzzled him.

Jared frowned. If he didn't know better, he would almost swear Paula had changed…that she was a different person altogether.

"How long will it take to get to…uh, Grace Harbor?" The question cut into Jared's chaotic thoughts, and he turned to find Paula in the doorway.

"It depends on the traffic and how many stops we make for the baby. All being well, we should get home sometime late tonight," he told her.

"Then I really think Nicky should be in a proper car seat."

"Fine. If the store you mentioned does in fact exist, we'll stop and buy one."

"Thank you," Faith said, relieved at his response. "The baby's stroller and my knapsack are by the front door," she told him, having already packed some clothes and her sketch pad, charcoal and pencils for the trip. "I still have to make up a few bottles and pack Nicky's diaper bag." Spinning away, she headed for the kitchen.

It was almost ten, and if Paula kept her promise, she would be calling very soon.

When Faith heard the front door being opened she

sighed with relief. Peeking out of the kitchen window, she watched Nicky's father carry the stroller and knapsack to his car.

Suddenly the silence was shattered by the telephone ringing. Faith quickly grabbed for the receiver, her pulse thundering loudly in her ears.

"Hello!"

"Faith? Hi! It's me."

"Paula! Oh…I'm so glad you called."

"Is something wrong?"

"Nicky's father's here," Faith said, her heart hammering wildly. "At least, he says he's Nicky's father. He arrived out of the blue this morning." She stretched the phone cord to enable her to look outside.

"Jared's there? You have to be joking!" Paula responded, shock in her voice.

"It's no joke, believe me."

"Yes…but, how—?" Paula broke off, then hurried on. "Describe him."

"Describe him?" Faith threw a panicked glance at Jared standing at the trunk of his car. "He's just like you said," she replied, and then briefly described him.

"That's Jared, all right," Paula said, her voice echoing over the wire.

"He says he's come to take Nicky home with him." Faith hurried on, all the while keeping an eye on Jared. "He's rude and arrogant, and he said something about you two having a deal. What kind of deal? What does he mean?"

"What did you tell him?" Paula asked, ignoring her question.

"I told him Nicky wasn't going anywhere without me. He keeps calling me Paula. Doesn't he know you have a twin sister?"

Paula was silent for a moment, and Faith could almost hear the wheels spinning in her sister's head as she plotted out a strategy. "Are you saying he thinks you're me?" Paula finally asked.

"Yes. I tried to set him straight, but he wouldn't listen." She watched as Jared closed the trunk and moved to the driver's door. "Maybe you should talk to him, tell him I'm only looking after Nicky until you get back."

"No...that's not a good idea."

"But surely you don't want me to just hand Nicky over to him, do you?" she went on, at a loss to understand her sister's lack of concern for her baby.

Her question was met with silence.

"Paula! Are you still there?"

"I'm still here."

"What's going on? There's something you're not telling me. Did you run away from this man? Was he physically abusing you?" she asked, as this possible explanation for her sister's strange behavior jumped into her mind.

"No! No...it's nothing like that," Paula assured her. "But he is very controlling. He told me I'd better forget about my acting career, and if I insisted on pursuing it, he'd fight me for sole custody of the baby, and do everything in his power to stop me from ever seeing Nicky again.''

Faith drew a startled breath. "Oh, how awful!" she responded, angered by Jared's arrogance and his dictatorial attitude. "What do you want me to do?"

"It would really help if I knew you were looking after Nicky. Will you do that for me?"

"I'll stay with him, I promise."

"And if you could play along with Jared—''

"Play along? But why?"

"If you tell him who you are, chances are he'll throw you out. Couldn't you just do it for a little while? For Nicky's sake. Just until I can talk to a lawyer and get some advice on how I should proceed," Paula pleaded.

"Oh…all right," Faith reluctantly agreed.

"Thanks sis. It really means a lot to me. Ah…listen, I've got to go. I'll be in touch. I know where to find you."

"Wait…" Faith began, but her sister had already hung up.

Faith slowly replaced the receiver. There had been something in her sister's voice, something Faith found infinitely disturbing.

"Who were you talking to?" Jared's appearance startled her. His question cut through her wayward thoughts, sending a guilty flush to her cheeks.

"No one…it was a wrong number." Faith managed to keep her voice even. "By the way, if we are stopping at the baby store, we should pick up a few tins of formula and another package of diapers," she added, in the hope of diverting his attention from the call.

"Aren't you carrying this doting-mother act a bit too far?" Jared commented.

"I don't know what you mean."

"All right, Paula, we'll play it your way," he said, with more than a hint of impatience. "Let's get this show on the road."

Faith closed the flap on the diaper bag and held it out to him. "I'll get Nicky."

As she handed Jared the bag, his fingers brushed against hers, sending a ripple of sensation scampering up her arm. Faith's gaze flew to meet his, but his stare was icy and unreadable, giving nothing away.

Faith turned away and headed down the hall to her bedroom, where Nicky lay on her bed, contentedly asleep. Gently gathering the baby into her arms and wrapping him in his baby blanket, Faith grabbed her keys from the dresser and left the room.

"Your friend is trusting indeed to give you your own set of keys," Jared commented after she'd finished locking the door.

Faith made no response as they crossed to the car. Jared opened the passenger door for her, and with great care she settled herself and her precious cargo into the leather bucket seat.

Reaching behind her for the strap of the seat belt, she suddenly found herself staring into a pair of dazzling blue eyes.

"Let me do that," Jared said and, pulling the seat belt, he leaned across to secure it.

Her breath locked in her throat as she shrank back against the upholstery. The faint smell of pine mingling with a darker, earthier scent that was decidedly male assailed her, and she felt her heart stumble against her ribs in response.

The instant Jared withdrew and closed the car door, Faith released the breath she was holding, and waited for her heart to find its usual rhythm, silently admonishing herself for reacting.

"Which way is the store?" Jared asked a few moments later as he eased the car out of the driveway.

"Take the first street on the left, and you'll see the parking lot in about three blocks," Faith answered, keeping her gaze firmly focused on the road ahead.

Half an hour later Nicky was safely ensconced in his brand-new car seat. Faith glanced at the clock on the dashboard, calculating that it would probably be another hour before Nicky would need changing and feeding.

Faith was silent as her companion drove under the sign indicating they were entering the freeway that would take them north. During her rather rushed conversation with Paula she hadn't even thought to ask her twin about Grace Harbor or its location.

The license plate on the car told her he was from Oregon, and with a name like Grace Harbor, it had to be somewhere on the coast. But much as she longed to ask Jared, she decided silence was the best policy.

Shifting her attention to the traffic on the busy freeway, she began to relax, enjoying the comfort and luxury his car offered. She even began to take pleasure in the ride, silently acknowledging that had everything to do with Jared's driving skills.

Unlike Glen, her ex-husband, Jared McAndrew was a highly competent driver, a driver who inspired confidence in his passengers, not anxiety. Jared appeared unperturbed by the poor driving habits of his fellow travelers. Instead of shouting and cursing at a driver who cut in front of him, he merely adjusted his speed, or calmly shifted lanes whenever the need arose.

Jared...Jared McAndrew. She let the name slide silently over her tongue. Solid and strong, she thought, much like the man himself.

Paula had said he was a controlling man, and Faith could easily relate and sympathize, having been married to a man who'd tried to rule her life.

But while Jared had been both rude and arrogant, demanding she hand over his son, and while his attitude toward the woman he believed had given birth to his son had been less than chivalrous, she found she couldn't fault him for the love and commitment he obviously felt toward his baby.

And what about the deal Jared had mentioned? What was that about? Stifling a sigh, Faith glanced into the back seat to check on Nicky, marveling at how good a baby he was and the fact that he was still asleep.

"Is he all right?" The softly spoken query came from the man at her side.

"Yes," Faith replied.

"He sleeps a lot. But I guess that's normal."

Faith heard the faint trace of anxiety in his voice. "Newborns do sleep a lot. But they can have their wakeful and fussy times, too. Erica had a fussy time—" She broke off abruptly, realizing with a sudden horror what she'd said.

"Erica? Who's Erica?" Jared threw her a puzzled glance.

Faith swallowed nervously. "Uh…Erica was just a kid I used to baby-sit," she improvised.

"Really," he said, though the skepticism in his voice told her he didn't believe a word she'd said. "As long as Nicky's asleep, I don't suppose you'd like to tell me why you ran off?"

His change of topic caught Faith totally off guard. She had no idea how to respond to his question.

"No," she said after a lengthy pause, praying silently he wouldn't pursue the matter. But the look Jared shot her told Faith he had other ideas.

"Did you leave because you'd changed your mind about our agreement?"

Glancing across at his profile, Faith noted the taut lines around his mouth as well as the stiffness of his jaw. Why did he look fearful of her reply?

What agreement? she wanted to ask, wishing again she'd insisted on a more detailed explanation from Paula before agreeing to participate in this charade.

"Cat got your tongue?" Jared flashed her a challenging look before returning his gaze once more to the road and the fast-moving traffic.

Faith said nothing as she stared down at his hands resting confidently on the steering wheel. It was then that she noticed the shiny gold band circling the fourth finger of his left hand. Her heart slammed against her breastbone in startled reaction, as the significance of the ring registered.

What bizarre game was her twin playing? Why hadn't Paula mentioned she and Jared McAndrew were married? Why hadn't Paula warned her she'd been cast in the role of counterfeit wife?

Chapter Three

The drive was pleasant and uneventful. They made several stops along the way to feed and change Nicky, including one outside Portland for supper.

As they waited for their hamburgers to arrive, Nicky began to fuss. Faith was surprised when Jared offered to hold him. He held her gaze in silent challenge, and, more than a little curious to see how he would deal with his fractious son, she handed him the baby.

She watched in admiration as Jared made caressing circles on his son's back. When he nestled Nicky into the curve of his neck and kissed the top of the baby's head, Faith's throat closed over with emotion, and tears gathered in her eyes.

Glen hadn't bothered to stick around long enough to see his daughter. But even before she discovered she was pregnant, she'd suspected him of having an affair.

She'd been midway through her pregnancy when the doctor had informed them there were major problems, that their baby would be born with multiple defects and with little chance of survival. Glen had taken his anger and frustration out on her, verbally berating her, blaming her for everything, before leaving for greener pastures.

Terminating the pregnancy hadn't been an option Faith had even considered, and so she'd struggled on alone, trying to come to terms with the harsh reality that her baby would not survive.

After Erica was born, Faith had insisted on taking the baby home, and the doctors had reluctantly agreed. The memories of those few precious days she'd had with her daughter had enabled her to work through some of her guilt and grief, and had eventually given her strength to go on.

Through lowered lashes Faith watched Jared attempt to quiet his son's urgent cries by gently rocking him and murmuring soft words. She admired his ability to remain calm in the face of Nicky's cries, and was impressed that he appeared to be totally unfazed by the stares from the other patrons of the restaurant.

When he smiled down at Nicky, the look of love Faith glimpsed in his eyes stirred old longings and brought an ache to her chest. Blinking back tears stinging her eyes, Faith concentrated on the hamburger the waitress had just brought. "It isn't too late." Jared's voice cut through the silence.

Frowning, she met his gaze. "I'm sorry, I don't understand."

"If you're having second thoughts, I can take you into Portland and drop you at the bus station," he said, his tone cool and indifferent.

Faith kept her voice steady. "I'm not leaving Nicky," she said, and caught the grudging respect that flashed in his eyes.

Later, after Nicky had fallen asleep in his arms, Jared had finished his own meal. Then, bundling the still-sleeping infant into his blanket, Jared paid the waitress and headed out to the car.

They continued their journey north in silence. Soon the warmth from the car's heater made Faith drowsy, and unable to fight off the wave of tiredness, she dozed off.

Almost an hour later the change in the car's rhythm roused her. Opening her eyes, she realized they were no longer on the freeway.

Darkness had descended, making it impossible to see the surrounding countryside. For a fleeting second a feeling of panic gripped her, sending her heart fluttering in her breast.

She had no idea where she was going. No idea what to expect once they reached Grace Harbor. And no idea whether she could, or should, in view of the ring on Jared's finger, go on pretending to be her twin.

Faith drew a steadying breath and turned to study

his silhouette. Undoubtedly aware that she'd awakened, he cast a quick glance in her direction. Even in the shadowed darkness of the car's interior she felt the impact of his gaze, and a ripple of sensation danced across her nerve endings.

She immediately turned her attention to the beam of headlights on the road ahead, silently acknowledging that he was indeed one of the most attractive men she'd ever encountered.

But looks could be deceiving. Glen Nelson had also been an attractive man, but behind his dynamic good looks there lurked a controlling and self-centered man.

Glen had been one of her instructors at the art college she'd attended. He was a well-known artist in his own right, so she'd been flattered by his attentions and by the compliments he'd afforded her work. Although he was twenty years her senior, she'd developed a crush on him, and when he asked her to accompany him to an art show in town, she'd eagerly accepted.

They'd had so many interests in common, or so she'd thought, and she'd felt comfortable and at ease with him. Six months later they'd had a quiet wedding, with only her parents and Glen's sister in attendance.

Almost from the moment the ceremony was over he'd changed, and it wasn't long before she came to the realization that having a wife much younger than himself fed his already overblown ego. He loved to show her off to his friends and colleagues as if she were a trophy, insensitive and uncaring of his wife's feelings.

Annoyed at the route her thoughts had taken, Faith closed the door on her memories, and suddenly through a break in the trees she glimpsed an array of twinkling lights.

The trees at last thinned out to reveal a peaceful little community she guessed must be Grace Harbor. Her gaze slid beyond the lights to what appeared to be ribbons of silver shimmering and undulating in the moonlight.

The ocean! Of course! She had to be looking at the powerful and magnificent Pacific Ocean.

"Oh…how beautiful," she exclaimed.

Her comment drew Jared's gaze. "I thought you hated the ocean," he said dryly.

Faith silently admonished herself for her lapse. What Jared said was true. Ever since Paula had fallen out of a sailboat during a storm when they were teens, nearly drowning in the process, she'd detested the ocean.

"Uh…I was just admiring the view," Faith muttered, reminding herself that while she and her twin were almost identical in appearance, their preferences and personalities had often been in opposing camps.

"Admiring the view…" Jared repeated, his tone mocking. "I guess there's a first time for everything."

Faith heard the underlying skepticism in his voice and wondered at the animosity and cynicism he continually directed toward her, or more accurately toward Paula, his wife and the mother of his child.

There had been times throughout the long drive north she'd been tempted to blurt out the truth, to tell Jared she wasn't Paula. But each time she'd glanced at his unsmiling and forbidding profile, she'd felt her courage evaporate.

She had to keep reminding herself of Jared's plan to fight for sole custody of Nicky, and his threat to deprive Paula of her son. These were reasons enough for her to continue with the deception, at least until Paula contacted a lawyer.

And while Faith didn't totally agree with or approve of the role she was being forced to play, she wanted to give her sister the benefit of the doubt and trust that Paula had the baby's best interests at heart.

Faith glanced at the man beside her. His concern for his infant son seemed genuine, but she reminded herself how easily Glen had disguised his controlling nature behind a charming smile.

Besides, it would serve no real purpose to reveal her true identity, and would undoubtedly result in Jared asking…no, demanding that she leave. And Faith knew she could no more abandon Nicky or renege on the promise she'd made to her twin than fly to the moon.

Suddenly they made a right turn, bringing Faith's attention back to the passing scene. She scanned the houses spread out along the street, noting that the car was climbing a steep hill. She wished it weren't so dark so she'd have a better view of the area. At the crest of the hill Jared made another turn, and they proceeded to the end of the road where the houses seemed larger and the lots spread farther apart.

Moments later Jared swung the car into a driveway, and as he slowed to a halt a light on the building came on, its brightness effectively blinding her.

Faith shielded her eyes, and as she adjusted to the light she noted the large double garage doors directly in front of her. Jared opened them electronically.

"Will Nick need feeding again before you put him to bed?" Jared asked as he drove the car into the garage.

"Possibly. But he might settle down and go back to sleep."

Jared switched off the engine, and in the dim lighting of the car's interior she turned to him. His gaze held hers captive for several long seconds. Suddenly a random thought dropped into Faith's mind, causing her heart to stumble in instant panic.

In her role of counterfeit wife, would she have to carry this crazy deception into the bedroom?

A rush of heat raced through her. Tearing her gaze away from Jared's, she reached for the door handle, calmly telling herself she would simply insist on sleeping in Nicky's room.

Besides, she quickly rationalized, if Jared's anger and hostility toward her was anything to go by, she doubted he'd put up an argument.

After opening the rear door of the car, she undid

the straps holding Nicky securely in place and gently eased him from the car seat. He stirred and whimpered a little in protest, then sighed and settled against her breast.

Faith closed the car door and turned to see Jared, the diaper bag slung over his shoulder, unlocking the door that led into the house.

With an air of confidence she was far from feeling, she caught up with him and followed him inside. When he stopped to flick on several light switches she almost collided with him.

Moments later she found herself in a spacious, brightly lit kitchen. In the center of the kitchen stood a work island, and on it a crystal fruit bowl containing a very ripe banana. With one quick glance Faith took in the pristine white cupboards and the burgundy-colored countertop. Blinds, the exact same shade as the counter, covered the windows above the sink.

Jared dropped the diaper bag on the counter and turned to her. "Why don't you take Nick to the nursery. I'll warm his bottle and bring it upstairs." He opened a cupboard next to the sink and retrieved a glass bowl.

"Uh...okay." Her gaze darted to the doorway on her left and the darkness beyond, then across the expanse of kitchen to another doorway. Which way were the stairs?

Nicky started to whimper, and Faith felt her pulse pick up speed. Before she could make a move, Jared turned to her once more.

"Is something wrong?" he asked, a frown creasing his handsome features.

"No," she assured him, but she made no move to leave. Nicky's whimpers changed to cries. "I need the diaper bag, that's all," she quickly improvised. "I'll change him first."

"Fine." Jared flipped open the diaper bag and extracted the last full bottle of formula. Picking the bag off the counter, he held it out to her.

Faith hesitated, wondering how she could get Jared to show her the way to the nursery.

"Uh…listen…why don't you take Nicky upstairs and change him?" she blurted out, and noted the flicker of surprise that came and went in his eyes. "If you don't want to…" Faith let the words trail off, silently praying he'd rise to the challenge.

Jared held her gaze for another long second as if trying to see inside her head. A flash of something, distrust perhaps, danced briefly in his eyes before he spoke. "I'll do it," he said.

Deftly slinging the diaper bag onto his shoulder, he closed the gap between them. As he lifted Nicky out of her arms the back of his hand brushed her breast, sending a jolt of electricity right to her toes.

Faith swayed a little and her breath caught in her throat in startled reaction. To her relief, Jared was already moving through the darkened doorway to her left. With a flick of a switch the hall light came on, revealing the stairs.

Slowly releasing the breath she was holding, Faith tried to convince herself that regardless of the fact the kitchen floor was covered with ceramic tiles, the jolt she'd just experienced had been nothing more than static electricity.

Alone, she surveyed the kitchen once more, and in an attempt to familiarize herself with its layout opened several doors and quickly scanned the contents.

She filled the bowl with hot water and placed Nicky's bottle in it to warm. Feeling sure Jared would be too involved changing the baby to notice how long she was taking, she decided to explore the lower floor.

Adjoining the kitchen was a midsize formal dining room with a beautiful oak table and eight ornate chairs. A large glass china cabinet displaying dishes and other china ornaments adorned one wall, while on the outside wall there was a set of elegant French doors. Tempted as she was to venture outside, Faith didn't linger.

From the dining room, there were two wide steps leading down to a sunken living room. The far wall was taken up entirely by a granite fireplace, and grouped in front of it were a dark green leather couch, matching love seat and a cream-colored brocade easy chair.

Faith's exploration was cut short by a muffled sound, coming from upstairs. Scurrying back across the thick, sand-colored carpet, she removed Nicky's bottle from the warm water, quickly dried it off and headed for the stairs.

On reaching the top of the curved stairway, Faith

glanced to her right. She could see three doors, each one standing open. She listened for a moment for a cry or a whimper that would direct her to the nursery.

She walked toward the first doorway, and as she approached, she heard the faint strains of a lullaby coming from within.

Jared sat in the chair gently rocking his son, softly humming along with the lullaby playing on the music box hanging on the end of the crib.

A soft sound caught Jared's attention and he glanced around to see Paula standing in the doorway.

Jared eased himself from the rocker and carried Nicky to the crib. As he tucked a tiny blanket around his son, he felt his heart swell with love. Nicky was home where he belonged, and nothing else mattered.

"He fell asleep," Jared said, turning to face her. "I guess he wasn't hungry after all."

"He'll probably be awake and very hungry sometime in the next hour. I'd better make up some more bottles. This is the last one," she said, indicating the one she'd brought with her.

"I'll give you a hand," Jared said.

"Thanks, but I can manage."

Jared crossed to the doorway, managing with difficulty to keep his anger in check.

"I said I'd give you a hand," he repeated. "I'll need to know how to make up Nicky's bottles, because we both know it's only a matter of time before you'll be on the first bus to L.A."

"No—" Faith protested, retreating into the hallway.

"I don't know what your game is, Paula, or why you came back here," Jared said, keeping his voice low. "I see you've even discarded the ring I gave you. Cramping your style, was it?" His tone held more than a hint of sarcasm. "I want you to listen and listen well," he continued. "Nicky is staying here with me. That was the deal we made. Remember?"

He held her gaze, daring her to deny what he'd said, but all he could see in the depths of her emerald green eyes was a look of pain and sorrow, a look that tugged strangely at his heart.

It was an act. The emotions he was seeing weren't real. She's an actress, he reminded himself, and a damned good one.

But he couldn't quite shake the feeling that there was something different about Paula, something he couldn't quite put his finger on.

"I'm staying," Faith said, her tone defiant. "How often do I have to say it before you believe me?" she asked, ignoring his comment about the ring.

Tension crackled between them like a living, breathing thing and suddenly Jared found himself fighting an almost overwhelming urge to haul her into his arms and cover her mouth with his.

But before he could follow through on the startling impulse, the phone rang, shattering the tension arcing between them.

Jared cursed under his breath. "Excuse me."

Spinning away, he hurried toward his bedroom, not sure whether he was relieved or annoyed by the timely interruption.

Crossing to his bedside table, he grabbed the receiver on the fourth ring. "Hello!" He practically spat the greeting into the mouthpiece.

"McAndrew! Greg Dunsford here."

"Greg! Hi," Jared responded. In all the excitement of locating Paula and Nicky, Jared had forgotten about the private detective he'd hired to track them down.

"I thought I'd better call and bring you up to date," the detective said. "Did you get the message I left on your answering machine last night?"

"Message? No...what message?" Jared asked. He hadn't had time to check them yet.

"A couple of hours after I called you last night to tell you I'd found her, she took off again. I followed the taxi to the San Francisco airport and called you from there—"

"I don't understand. What do you mean, you followed her to the airport?" Jared asked, frowning.

"She left the address I gave you in San Francisco and hopped a cab to the airport," Greg Dunsford repeated. "But this time she didn't take the baby with her."

"Didn't what?" Jared ran a hand through his hair, growing more confused by the second.

"I managed to get a ticket on the same flight, then I called and left you a message," he continued.

"Once we got to L.A., I had trouble keeping up with her. I kept losing her in the traffic."

"Losing her? What the hell are you talking about?" Jared asked, totally lost now.

"I figured she'd be heading downtown and got lucky after I checked out a few places. I'm happy to report I've picked up her trail again," he went on. "She's here in L.A., staying at the Plaza."

"Who's in L.A.?" Jared countered. His head was spinning, and he was beginning to wonder if he'd somehow walked into the middle of an old vaudeville comedy routine.

"Paula Preston, of course. The woman you hired me to find," the detective replied.

Chapter Four

Jared slowly replaced the receiver, his thoughts in chaos. He sank onto his bed and, elbows on his knees, bent forward and tunneled both hands through his hair. What the hell was going on?

Resting his head in his hands for a moment, he struggled to make sense of it all. Greg must have made a mistake. Paula was downstairs.

The woman Greg had followed to L.A. had to have been someone who looked like Paula—her actor friend and most likely the owner of the house in San Francisco. Realizing someone was tailing her, Paula had probably asked her friend to impersonate her as a means of throwing Greg off the scent and buying herself some time.

It was the only logical explanation. Wanting to cover all the bases, however, Jared had instructed Greg to keep the woman he thought was Paula under surveillance and report back in a few days with an update.

In the meantime, curiosity, along with a need to have his suspicions confirmed, prompted Jared to make some inquiries of his own concerning the owner of the house in San Francisco.

Reaching for the phone, he placed a call to his college buddy Damian DeMarco, a detective in the San Francisco Police Department who he knew liked to work night shift.

"Detective DeMarco." His friend's familiar husky voice came down the wires. "How can I help you?"

"Hey, DeMarco! Haven't they promoted you to captain yet?" Jared teased.

"Jared! Hey, good buddy! How goes it?" his friend replied. "Are you calling to tell me you're here in town?"

"No, I'm afraid not," Jared replied. "I'm calling to ask a favor."

DeMarco chuckled. "I might have known. Okay. Fire away," he said.

"If I give you an address in San Francisco, could you check the owner out for me, find out everything you can?" Jared asked.

"Is this for a case you're working on?" the detective asked.

"In a way," Jared hedged, and proceeded to give him the address.

"I suppose I could make some discreet inquiries, if that's what you want," DeMarco replied. "It's quiet here tonight. I'll get on it right away and give you a call tomorrow.''

"Great. Oh…would you call me at my office,'' Jared said. "And thanks, buddy. I owe you one.''

Satisfied he'd done all he could, Jared hung up.

Faith stood in the kitchen listening for the sounds of footsteps that would tell her Jared was off the phone. After he'd hurried toward the bedroom down the hall to answer the telephone's summons, she'd taken the opportunity to peek into the bedroom directly opposite the nursery.

The room was large and spacious with an adjoining bathroom, and it was with some relief that Faith noted the general state of upheaval, an upheaval that told her someone had recently been occupying the room.

Venturing farther inside, Faith opened the closet door to discover an assortment of dresses, blouses and pants, some of them maternity wear, clothes she guessed belonged to her sister.

Faith felt reasonably sure Paula had been sleeping in the guest bedroom, and she could only assume that in the late stages of her pregnancy and out of consideration for her husband, Paula had moved out of the master bedroom.

For Faith it was a reprieve, of sorts.

On returning to the kitchen, she'd busied herself making up a batch of bottles for Nicky. But as the minutes slowly ticked by with no sign of Jared, she began to worry and wonder. Could the caller have been Paula? Or perhaps Paula's lawyer?

"Sorry, I didn't mean to take so long."

Faith drew a startled breath as Jared's voice cut through her musings. She tensed, waiting expectantly for him to announce that he knew her true identity, followed by an angry demand for her to leave.

"I just locked up the garage and brought in your knapsack," he said. "I left it at the foot of the stairs. You've finished making up Nicky's bottles, I see."

"Yes," Faith responded.

"Fine. You can show me how it's done next time," he said. "I don't know about you, but I could use a drink." Jared sauntered across the floor toward her. "Care to join me?"

Caught off guard by the invitation, Faith darted him a nervous glance.

"Ah...no, thank you," she said. "Nicky will be awake soon, and I'm rather tired. I think I'll just go up to bed." As soon as the words were out she felt her pulse gather speed, wondering if Jared would think she meant she'd be waiting in his bed...their bed.

Flustered, she could feel a telltale blush begin to invade her cheeks, and hurriedly she backed away from his advancing figure, hoping he wouldn't notice.

Jared saw the color seep into her face and noted, too, the way she deliberately sidestepped him. Frowning, he reached up to open the cupboard above the fridge and extracted a half-empty bottle of Napoleon brandy.

"You don't have to worry about Nicky," he said as he opened another cupboard and removed a brandy snifter. "I'll take care of him when he wakes up."

"There's no need," she quickly assured him. Rounding the work island, she widened the gap between them. "I really don't mind...." Her voice trailed off.

"Aren't you taking this doting-mother routine a little too far?" Jared's tone was challenging and his gaze zeroed in on her.

"I...I don't know what you mean," she responded, quickly breaking eye contact with him, but not before he'd seen the flicker of panic that danced briefly in her green eyes.

What on earth was going on? Jared silently wondered. Paula actually looked disconcerted. And that wasn't something he'd witnessed very often, if ever.

Jared studied her for a moment. Something was missing. Dropping his gaze, he twisted the cap on the brandy and poured himself a small amount.

Lifting the glass to his nose, he swirled the gold liquid around. As the fumes rose to greet him, he suddenly realized what was different about her.

She wasn't wearing any makeup. There was no mascara to darken her incredibly long lashes, no blusher to accentuate those classic cheekbones and no dark red lipstick to emphasize her sexy mouth. He was surprised he hadn't noticed it before.

During the time she'd stayed with him, he'd learned a great deal about her, and for the most part he hadn't been impressed. Self-absorbed and selfish came to mind.

She'd never lifted a finger to help around the house. He'd had to cook and clean as well as listen to her constant complaints; complaints about how boring a life he led, about how she hated Grace Harbor and about her expanding waistline.

When she wasn't grumbling about how boring everything was, she'd spent her time reading the latest gossip and scandals in the tabloids.

He'd thought when he started painting the nursery she'd show some interest. He'd been wrong. He'd chosen the color scheme and picked out a crib and dresser, as well as the change table and other sundries.

He'd bought several books about pregnancy, books that described in detail the growth and development of a baby through each wondrous month. While he'd devoured every word, fascinated by the miracle he'd helped create, she'd simply ignored them.

There had been times he'd wondered what he'd ever seen in her, how he'd been attracted to someone so superficial and self-centered.

Jared turned to look at the woman standing across the room. His gaze lingered on her face. Her skin glowed with a natural, healthy shine and her heart-shaped face had an appeal that was hard to ignore. Annoyed, he tossed back a mouthful of brandy.

What he still failed to understand was why Paula was here.

"You know, you don't have to pretend with me," he said. "You don't have to continue with this charade on my account."

"Ch-charade...what charade?" she responded.

Jared heard the faint quiver in her voice, and for the second time in as many minutes he glimpsed uncertainty in her eyes.

"We had a deal, remember," he said, suddenly deciding to goad her. "You agreed to grant me sole custody of our son. And don't tell me you ran off because you had a change of heart, because I don't believe it for a minute," he taunted. "Come on, Paula. Why don't you just tell me why you're here. What's in it for you? Is it money you want? What game are you playing?"

He watched the blood drain from Paula's face. An array of emotions he couldn't quite decipher flitted across her ashen features.

His intention had been to provoke an angry response, goad her into retaliating, in the hope she might show her hand and reveal something... anything.

Instead, she'd flinched at his angry words, almost as if he'd physically struck her. Her green eyes had darkened to jade as pain and bewilderment flashed in their depths, emotions he'd never thought her capable of feeling.

"Deals can be broken," Paula said after a lengthy, tension-filled pause.

Her softly spoken words turned the blood in his veins to ice.

This couldn't be happening! Paula, who'd longed for the day when the baby would be born so she could leave Grace Harbor and return to her acting career, was standing before him with a look of determination in her eyes that left him reeling.

"What are you saying?" Jared managed to keep his tone even, and tried with difficulty to rein in the rage steadily building inside him. "Even if giving birth did awaken your maternal instincts, we both know it isn't going to last. Put it down to hormones, my dear, because I guarantee you in a week, maybe two, you'll be yearning to get back to the bright lights. How many times did you tell me the very thought of changing a dirty diaper or waking up in the middle of the night to tend to a crying, cranky, hungry baby made you break out in hives?"

"I was wrong," Paula replied in a clear voice. "I've done those things, and I survived. Besides, isn't it a woman's prerogative to change her mind?"

Stunned, Jared couldn't think of a thing to say.

"It's been a long day. I'm going to bed," she added, and without waiting for a reply, she walked from the room.

Jared stood like a statue carved out of ice staring after her departing figure. Was it really possible for a woman like Paula to change so dramatically, and in such a short time?

Much as he wanted to dismiss the notion, much as he longed to believe she was simply yanking his chain, there had been something in her voice and in her eyes he couldn't ignore.

He downed the remainder of his brandy. For a brief moment he was tempted to smash the glass into the sink, in an attempt to vent the rage coursing through him.

What he'd feared most had come to pass, and the reason Paula had returned with him was that she had indeed changed her mind. She wanted to keep Nicky after all!

Faith woke with a start, her heart hammering wildly in her breast. She sat up and glanced around at the menacing shadows in the unfamiliar room. Where was she? This wasn't her bedroom! This wasn't her bed!

The sound of a baby crying broke the silence, and the memory of the previous day came rushing back. Nicky!

Faith glanced at the digital clock radio on her bedside table. She read twelve-thirty. Shoving the bedcovers aside, she stood up and quickly crossed to the door.

She'd taken only one step into the dimly lit hallway when she collided with a solid, warm, half-naked man.

"Oh!" She staggered backward.

"I'm sorry! Are you all right?" Jared clasped her upper arms to steady her.

"Yes, thank you," Faith answered, though she felt oddly breathless. As her eyes adjusted to the shadowed darkness, she found herself staring at the smooth clean lines of Jared's muscled chest.

Her pulse skittered to a halt as she lifted her gaze to meet his, and in that heart-stopping second she felt a strong but unmistakable tug of attraction.

Suddenly the sound of Nicky's cries grew louder and more urgent. They reacted simultaneously and, like two clumsy clowns performing a slapstick routine, they bumped into each other a second time.

This time her hands were trapped against Jared's naked chest. Beneath her splayed fingers she could feel the warmth of his skin, its smooth texture, and at the prolonged contact a quicksilver jolt of response spiraled through her.

"Laurel and Hardy couldn't have done better," Jared said, humor lacing his voice. "Nicky will never get fed if we keep this up."

"Sorry," Faith mumbled, jerking free of his hold.

"Why don't you go downstairs and warm his bottle while I change him."

"Okay," Faith said, happy to comply, eager to put some distance between them.

Downstairs, she set the baby's bottle in the bowl with warm water, all the while recalling those moments on the landing.

It had been a long time since she'd felt the strength and comfort of a man's arms around her. She hadn't realized just how much she'd missed it until now.

Annoyed at the route her thoughts had taken, she

silently berated herself. She couldn't be attracted to Jared. The very idea was unthinkable.

Deliberately she switched her thoughts to their confrontation in the kitchen earlier and to Jared's startling comment about Paula agreeing to give him custody of Nicky.

It couldn't be true! Could it? Paula had told her Jared had been the one threatening to fight her for custody. One of them had to be lying. But which one?

Faith had lain awake for some time pondering the question. On reflection she had to acknowledge that she'd never expected to open her front door and find Paula on the doorstep with a newborn baby in tow.

Marriage and children hadn't been at the top of Paula's list of priorities, but the fact remained, Paula was married, and she was now the mother of a beautiful, healthy baby, and Faith couldn't bring herself to believe her twin would willingly agree to give up her child.

Whatever problems Paula and Jared faced in their marriage, it was obvious Nicky was the one who had the most to lose.

Faith decided her best course of action was to simply wait until she heard from Paula, and in the meantime avoid any further confrontations or close physical contact with Jared.

After testing the bottle, Faith headed upstairs.

Jared, with an increasingly fretful Nicky in his arms, was pacing the room. A look of relief came into his eyes when she appeared.

"He's starving. Your timing is perfect," he said as he reached for the bottle. When her fingers brushed his, it was all Faith could do to ignore the faint tremor of awareness that shimmied up her arm.

"He slept longer than I thought he would," Faith commented as Jared walked to the rocking chair and sat down.

Mesmerized, Faith lingered near the door watching Jared settle Nicky into a comfortable position against his chest. In a matter of seconds those familiar sucking sounds could be heard as the baby eagerly drank from the bottle.

"You don't have to stay and supervise," Jared told her in a low voice. "I assure you I'm quite capable of feeding and burping my son."

Faith met his gaze. "I wasn't—" she began.

"Or are you hanging around for another reason?" he asked, his gaze drifting over her scanty attire.

Her breath caught in her throat at the blatant sexual undertone in his voice. He thought she was Paula, his wife, and as she glanced down at the cotton nightshirt that reached midway to her thighs, she realized she had only herself to blame for the speculative gleam she could see in his eyes.

"I wasn't...you can't..." she stumbled to a halt, heat suffusing her face.

Amusement tugged at the corner of his mouth, and silently she berated herself for reacting. Without another word, she withdrew, but not before she saw a glint of triumph flicker briefly in his eyes.

Five hours later Faith reached out to shut off the music coming from the clock radio. This time she remembered exactly where she was, and she lay listening for a sound that would tell her if either Jared or Nicky was awake. The house was shrouded in silence.

After a quick shower, she dressed in the faded jeans and baggy sweater she'd worn the day before. Tying her hair back in a loose ponytail, she tiptoed across the hall to the nursery.

Smiling, she gazed down at Nicky's sleeping figure. He hadn't awakened again, but Faith felt sure he'd be awake any minute now. As she watched him, she felt her throat tighten with unshed tears and that familiar ache tug at her heart.

He was so beautiful. So perfect. So healthy. Faith wondered for a moment if Paula truly realized how fortunate she was to have given birth to a healthy baby.

Nicky stretched and started to whimper. Before he began crying in earnest, Faith reached into the crib and lifted him into her arms. She cuddled him against her shoulder, and in soft, whispered tones she shushed him.

After changing and feeding Nicky, Faith popped him back into his crib and headed to the kitchen. Pulling out three eggs, a loaf of bread and a package of coffee, she started breakfast. It wasn't long before the aroma of coffee brewing filled the kitchen.

"Have you fed Nicky already?" The sound of

Jared's voice startled Faith and she spun around to face him.

Her breath snagged in her throat at the sight of him, his hair still wet from the shower, his jaw freshly shaved, his long lean body draped in a gray three-piece business suit, white shirt and striped tie. He looked like a model on the cover of a *GQ* magazine, and it was all Faith could do to find her voice.

"Yes," she replied, resolutely reminding herself that Jared was her sister's husband. And that men with good looks, easy charm and incredible sex appeal were not to be trusted.

"Is that coffee I smell? What are you doing?" Jared asked as he dropped his briefcase on the kitchen table.

"Making breakfast. Would you like a poached egg?"

Jared blinked, his surprise obvious. "You're offering to make breakfast for me?"

Faith instantly realized she'd made a mistake. She knew Paula's cooking skills were limited, and from Jared's reaction it wasn't hard to deduce that Paula hadn't been in the habit of cooking breakfast for her husband.

"I thought I'd try," she replied cautiously.

"Thanks. I'll pick up something on my way to the office."

"Fine," Faith said, turning back to the stove, aware of the sideways glance Jared threw her way. Heart pounding, she focused her attention on breaking the egg and dropping it gently into the simmering water.

She'd be glad when he left for work, she thought absently, finding his presence much too disturbing.

"So, Paula, tell me, how long are you planning to stick around? Will you still be here when we get back?"

Faith bristled at his tone. "Of course I'll be here. I wouldn't leave Nicky."

"Ah...but, you see, that isn't the issue, because Nicky's coming with me."

Startled, Faith turned to meet his amused gaze, her breakfast forgotten. "What?" she said.

"Was I speaking a foreign language?" he asked, a hint of impatience in his voice. "I said Nicky's coming to the office with me," Jared repeated, his blue eyes daring her to argue. "You don't think after your last little disappearing act I'd be foolish enough to leave my son here with you, do you?"

Chapter Five

Faith inhaled sharply at Jared's words. Surprise ricocheted through her, but she held his gaze, determined not to let him see just how much he'd shaken her.

"You can't mean that." She pushed the words past lips that were dry.

"Get real, Paula. We both know the minute I drive away you'll bundle Nicky up and hit the road again."

Faith swallowed. She couldn't argue, nor could she blame him for thinking the worst of her. But before she could respond, the telephone started ringing.

Jared spun away and grabbed the receiver off the wall next to the fridge. "Hello! Yes, Sally. What's up?" He listened for a moment, and Faith watched as his expression swiftly underwent a change.

"You're right, I did forget about the meeting." Annoyance edged his voice. "No, don't cancel it. It took me months to get the two parties to agree to meet with me in the first place." He glanced down at his wristwatch. "I can still be there in time if I leave right now. Thanks for the reminder, Sally. I'll see you in the office later."

Jared replaced the receiver and crossed to the table. "How long will it take to get Nicky ready?" he asked as he opened his briefcase.

Faith glanced over at him in surprise. "You aren't taking Nicky with you to your meeting?"

"I don't have a choice, do I?" he answered, his tone impatient as he began to rearrange some files.

"Yes, you do. Leave Nicky here with me. It isn't fair to wake him up and drag him off at a moment's notice," she argued.

Jared dropped the folders back into his briefcase. "You must be joking!" His tone was scathing. "You vanish without a trace days before the baby's due, and you expect me to trust you not to run off with him again. I don't think so!"

Faith managed to keep her expression neutral, determined not to react to his outburst, while her mind raced at his revelation.

"I'm thinking of Nicky," she said, ignoring the look of disbelief that flashed in his eyes. "It isn't fair to disrupt his schedule. He's just a baby. How do you expect to take care of him and conduct a meeting at the same time? I doubt your clients will want to listen to him cry," she added for emphasis.

Jared hesitated. She was right. From the books he'd read on the subject of infant care he knew how important it was to maintain a schedule, especially at this early stage in the baby's life. Taking Nicky to his office might have worked in another instance but not now when his clients were in the midst of a bitter divorce, fighting over custody of their two-year-old child. Nicky's presence wouldn't help matters in the least.

"What if I promise you Nicky and I will be here when you get back?"

Jared held her gaze for a long moment. Could he trust Paula to keep her word? She certainly sounded sincere, and her concern for Nicky appeared to be genuine.

"We'll be here. I promise," Faith repeated, obviously reading indecision on his face.

"All right." Jared relented, silently praying he wasn't making another mistake and Paula wasn't simply putting on an act. "But I'm going to call as soon as I get to the meeting, and then every hour on the hour after that. You'd better be here."

Faith heard the threat in his voice, and inwardly she shrank from it. During her three-year marriage to Glen, he had often used bullying tactics whenever she'd opposed him in some way. "I'll be here," Faith insisted quietly.

Jared snapped the lid of his briefcase closed. Without another word he turned and strode out of the kitchen. Faith heard the door leading to the garage close behind him, and minutes later the car's engine revved up.

With a sigh she reached for the pot on the stove. Her poached egg had turned to mush, and the toast, long since popped from the toaster, had grown cold. After cleaning out the pan, she went upstairs to check on Nicky and then returned to the kitchen.

Pouring herself a cup of coffee, she leaned back against the counter and let her mind replay their conversation. If Paula had run off only days before Nicky was born, she could well understand his unwillingness to trust her.

What could have prompted her twin to take such an action? she wondered. Her thoughts shifted to those moments in her driveway in San Francisco when Jared had crouched in front of the stroller. She understood now why he'd looked so dumbstruck. That had to have been the first time he'd set eyes on his son!

His rapt expression as he'd gazed at Nicky in the stroller had been heart-wrenchingly real, effectively softening those angry lines on his handsome face.

But the question remained. Why had Paula run away? It had to be connected with her career. There was no other explanation.

Besides, Paula had done something similar in her late teens. She'd borrowed their mother's credit card to buy a plane ticket to New York, and for forty-eight hours her parents had been frantic with worry. When she'd called it had been to excitedly tell them about the off-Broadway show she'd seen and how she'd waited several hours in the alley behind the theater to get the cast to autograph her program.

Faith shook her head. She doubted she'd ever understand what made her sister tick. But when Paula called again, Faith planned to ask a few pointed questions.

As if in tune to her thoughts, the phone rang, the shrill sound slicing into the silence. Faith froze. Could it be Paula?

On the second ring she jerked forward, sending the cooling coffee in her mug splashing over the rim onto her hands.

Setting the mug on the counter, she reached for a tea towel. She picked up the receiver on the fourth ring.

"Hello!" she said, a trifle breathlessly.

"What kept you?" Jared's deep voice, mixed with anger and relief, reverberated through the wires, sending a shiver through her.

"Nothing. I answered didn't I?" Faith replied, annoyed at his tone and at the leap her pulse had taken in response to his voice.

"But how do I know Nicky isn't sitting in his stroller right now ready to go? And how do I know you haven't called a cab to take you to the bus station the minute I hang up?" he went on, suspicion echoing in his voice.

Faith bit back the sigh hovering on her lips, wondering why she should care that he thought so little of her. "I made a promise, Jared, a promise I intend to keep."

There was silence for several seconds. "I'll call you in half an hour. Be there!" He promptly hung up.

Faith slowly replaced the receiver and turned her attention to cleaning up the coffee spill. She tidied the kitchen, then made her way upstairs to the nursery to check on Nicky.

Standing by the crib, she gazed down at the baby, watching the gentle rise and fall of his chest. Tears gathered in her eyes and emotion clogged her throat.

During Erica's short life Faith had spent a good deal of time watching her daughter sleep. She'd insisted on bringing Erica home, adamantly opposed to the doctor's suggestion to hook her up to machines simply to put off what they all knew to be inevitable.

Heartbreaking as those few days had been, Faith had never regretted her decision. She'd been able to hold her daughter and feed her, showering her with love and attention, then crying bitter, helpless tears when Erica's life had finally slipped away.

Brushing a stray tear from her cheek, Faith tiptoed from the room. She busied herself making her bed, rechecking the items left by her sister in the bedroom closet and small chest of drawers.

Faith peeked in on Nicky once more before venturing down the hall to Jared's room. She told herself what she was about to do wasn't snooping, nor was it really an invasion of privacy. By taking a look in Jared's bedroom she was simply attempting to find out a little more about the man her sister had married, the man who was Nicky's father.

The master bedroom was large and spacious, with a king-size bed against one wall, a work desk with a computer on another and an enormous old-fashioned mirrored wardrobe on the wall behind the door.

The room was tidy, the bed made. The walls were painted a pale blue, and the duvet cover and drapes were patterned in contrasting shades of blue and green. A beautiful hardwood floor was strewn with braided oval rugs—one moss green, one navy blue, one a dark burgundy. On the nightstand beside the bed sat a telephone and clock radio, and above the mahogany headboard was a watercolor painting of a wild seascape.

The smell of pine and mint swirled around her mixing with yet another scent, unmistakably masculine. A ripple of sensation scampered across her nerve endings, making Faith instantly regret her decision to investigate Jared's room.

Just as she started to leave, the phone rang. It had to be Jared checking up on her again. Crossing over to the bed, she picked up the receiver. "Hello!"

"Just checking!" Jared's voice hummed through the lines.

"I'm still here," Faith responded, feeling her pulse falter as his masculine scent, stronger now that she was closer to the bed where he slept, assailed her from all sides.

"Keep it that way," Jared said before hanging up.

As Faith replaced the receiver she heard sounds of Nicky stirring and gladly hurried from Jared's room.

Returning to the nursery, she wound up a music box hanging from the end of the crib, and while Nicky lay listening to the lullaby, she half filled the small bathtub with warm water and set it on the change table. She wasn't sure what his reaction would be. She thought he might cry, but when he started to move his tiny legs in the water, she smiled. Speaking soft assurances to him, she gently poured handfuls of water over his body.

A few minutes later she lifted him out of the bath and wrapped him in a soft towel. After patting him dry, she laid him in the crib while she checked through the assortment of baby clothes in the dresser drawers.

She wondered if Paula had organized the nursery and bought the baby clothes, but somehow she couldn't quite picture her twin shopping for anyone other than herself. That left Jared. Could he have done it all? The idea intrigued her.

Faith dressed Nicky in a pale blue sleeper with a bunny motif on the back. Leaving him in his crib, she headed downstairs.

Hearing the phone ring again, Faith reached for the receiver. "I'm still here," she said without preamble.

"Excuse me?"

"I'm sorry! I thought—" Faith broke off, quickly realizing the caller wasn't Jared after all.

"Paula? You're back! That's wonderful!" said the woman on the other end of the line.

"Ah…well, yes. I mean—"

"It's Maggie. Maggie O'Connor. Remember me?" she asked cheerfully.

"Yes…of course," Faith answered, hoping she sounded more confident than she felt.

"Is Jared home?"

"No. He had an early meeting this morning."

"When did you get back? Did Jared fetch you and the baby?"

"Yes, last night," Faith said, silently wondering just what Jared had told his friends and neighbors about the disappearance of his pregnant wife.

"He's been so worried about you and anxious to have the two of you home. I must admit we were surprised when we heard you'd decided at the last minute to go to your mother's to have the baby."

Faith remained silent. So that's how Jared had explained it.

"How are you? And more important, how's the baby?" Maggie asked, oblivious to the turmoil she was creating.

Faith drew a steadying breath. "I'm fine, thank you. Ah…Nicky's fine, too," she added, wishing the conversation would end.

"Nicky. Is that the name you finally chose?"

"Actually it's Nicholas."

"I like it," Maggie said. "Jared said you couldn't make up your minds. Listen, I was just on my way out. Would it be all right to pop over and see Nicky?''

''Ah…well, that is—uh…sure, why not…'' Faith let her words trail off, unable to think of a reason to dissuade her.

''Wonderful! See you in a few minutes.''

Faith sagged against the counter, her heart hammering wildly. Why couldn't it have been Jared on the phone? Her mind raced. Perhaps she should call him. But how could she? She didn't know the number of his office. And besides, he wasn't at the office, he was at a meeting.

Turning, Faith ran a hand through her hair trying to quell the panic rising inside. How well had Maggie known her twin? Would Maggie be able to tell she wasn't Paula? Perhaps she'd notice Faith wasn't wearing a wedding ring. If Maggie did comment, Faith decided she'd simply say her ring needed resizing.

Faith tried to stay calm, reassuring herself with the thought that if Paula hadn't told Jared she had a twin sister, it was unlikely she'd told anyone.

When the doorbell rang ten minutes later Faith pinned a smile on her face. Crossing her fingers, she took a deep, steadying breath.

''Paula! Hi! You look great!'' The young woman standing in the doorway smiled warmly at Faith. Maggie O'Connor tossed back the hood of her jacket to reveal shoulder-length dark hair and eyes the color of milk chocolate. ''Jared must be over the

moon now he has you and the baby back home,"
Maggie continued.

"Ah...yes. Thank you," Faith responded, not
knowing what else to say.

"You remember Dylan junior?" Maggie said,
grinning down at the baby sitting in the stroller.

"Of course," she quickly improvised, gazing
down at the little boy.

"Hasn't he grown?" Maggie said.

"He sure has," Faith responded, crouching to
smile at the baby.

"He's only five months old, but he weighs in at
twenty pounds and counting," Maggie said proudly.

"He's gorgeous." Faith's tone was sincere, and
she smiled as Dylan waved his hands at her and
giggled.

"Is Nicky asleep?" Maggie asked.

"I think so," Faith said. "Ah...won't you come
in?"

"Thanks. I'm dying to see him," Maggie went
on excitedly. Bending down, she lifted Dylan from
his stroller and followed Faith into the foyer.

"Nicky's upstairs in his crib, but you're welcome
to take a peek," Faith offered, hoping to distract
Maggie from asking any more questions.

Maggie took the bait, her smile widening. "Could
we?"

Faith led the way to the nursery. To Maggie's
delight Nicky was awake, and while Faith changed
his diaper, Maggie chatted to her, asking her about
her labor and how the birth had gone.

Keeping her answers as brief and as vague as she could, Faith described her own not too taxing labor, and after answering a few more questions, she turned the conversation to baby Dylan. Maggie readily complied.

"Would you like a cup of coffee?" Faith asked a little while later as they made their way downstairs.

"Maybe another time," Maggie said. "Dylan and I are on our way to the grocery store," she explained.

"Really?" Faith said. "We need a few groceries. Jared forgot to stock up," she added.

"Why don't you come with us," Maggie suggested. "Or does Nicky need to be fed?"

Faith hesitated and glanced at the clock. It was a little after ten. "He should be fine for another hour or so."

Her concern wasn't for Nicky but for Jared, who'd be calling soon to check up on her. Still, they did need groceries. "We'll come to the store with you, if that's all right," Faith said brightly, deciding the trip to the store would also afford her an opportunity to acquaint herself a little with Grace Harbor.

Jared listened in silent fury to the sound of the phone ringing in his house. On the sixth ring the answering machine kicked in and, gritting his teeth, he slammed down the receiver.

Damn her! He couldn't believe it! After all her promises, she'd skipped out! He'd been a fool to trust her. A fool to believe anything she'd said. Only, there had been something in her voice, in her eyes…

She couldn't have gotten far. And this time when he found her…

Jared grabbed his briefcase and strode into the outer office. Sally Cooper, his girl Friday, was talking on the phone. She put her hand over the mouthpiece.

"Mr. McAndrew, there's a Detective DeMarco on the line," she said. "Do you want to take the call?"

Jared stopped. He'd forgotten about his call to Damian.

"Yes, I'll take it." Jared made a U-turn into his office. Punching the button flashing on the phone, he lifted the instrument once more. "DeMarco! Hi! What did you find out?" he asked without preamble.

"Not much. At least, nothing remotely suspicious or criminal."

"Give me what you got," Jared said, biting back a sigh of frustration.

"This morning I paid a visit to the address you gave me, but the house was empty. I talked to a neighbor, who told me the house is owned by Faith Nelson. It was part of her divorce settlement. And by the sounds of things, she's well rid of the guy."

"Faith Nelson?" Jared repeated. The name meant nothing to him. "Anything else?"

"According to her neighbor, Ms. Nelson is an illustrator of children's books. The ex-husband is an artist. Oh…get this, she was four months pregnant when he walked out. Apparently the baby died less than a week after it was born.''

Jared silently digested this information, trying to decide whether or not it was in any way significant.

"Is that all?" Jared asked.

"Afraid so," his friend replied. "Wait! I don't know if this is important or not, but the neighbor mentioned that she'd seen Ms. Nelson's sister arrive with a baby two nights ago. By the way, did you know they're identical twins?"

Jared stopped breathing. Twins! Suddenly it all made sense. But Paula had never mentioned having any family. He'd been under the impression she didn't have any relatives. If Paula had an identical twin...then...

"Hey, buddy, are you still there?" Damian's voice cut through his chaotic thoughts.

Jared released the breath trapped in his lungs. "I'm still here."

"Do you want me to keep digging?"

"No, but thanks, Damian."

"Any time," his friend replied.

Jared slowly replaced the receiver. Twins! Identical twins! Incredible!

He cast his mind back to those moments when he'd first set eyes on the baby stroller. He'd hardly given Paula more than a cursory glance. He'd been too caught up in the joy of finding his son safe and sound.

On reflection, her startled reaction to his appear-

ance and her subsequent behavior had puzzled him
a little, but at the time he'd brushed it aside.

The private detective he'd hired had obviously
tracked Paula to her sister's house, where Paula had
left the baby in her sister's care before heading to
L.A.

And the woman Jared had confronted, the woman
who'd accompanied him to Grace Harbor and was
meantime taking care of his son, was in all likelihood Paula's twin sister.

Jared glanced down at the name he'd hurriedly
scribbled on a pad on his desk. Faith Nelson.

She'd fooled him completely, which could only
mean she was in cahoots with Paula. Ripping the
sheet of paper off the notepad, he headed into the
outer office.

"Sally. There's something I have to do. Can you
hold down the fort?"

Chapter Six

Jared drove home as fast as the law allowed. He'd decided to check out the house first, hoping Paula—or Faith—had been too busy giving Nicky a bath to answer his earlier call. Reaching the house, he found the door unlocked. Once inside, he took the stairs two at a time.

"Paula? Are you up here?" he called as he strode toward the nursery.

His question was met with silence. The nursery was empty. Spinning, he exited and descended once more to the main floor, where everything appeared the same as it had that morning. Completing a circuit of the dining room and living room, he returned to the front entranceway. What he'd feared and suspected was true. They were gone.

Muttering to himself about his own stupidity in trusting her, Jared hurried out to his car. Just as he was about to climb into the driver's seat he noticed two women walking along the street, each pushing a baby stroller.

He recognized his friend Maggie's familiar features immediately, and beside her... A feeling of relief washed over him when he saw Paula. No, he silently amended, the other woman's identity had yet to be confirmed.

With his heart thundering in his chest, he watched the women approach. Judging by the way Maggie was chatting and smiling, it was clear she believed the woman with her was Paula. But Maggie had met Paula only a couple of times. She'd repeatedly tried to befriend her, but Paula had declined all Maggie's invitations.

Jared frowned. From this distance the woman looked exactly like Paula. Could DeMarco's information about Paula having a twin sister be wrong? It was time to find out.

"Hello, ladies." Jared walked around the car to meet them.

"Jared! How nice to see you," Maggie greeted him with a smile. "Paula didn't say anything about you coming home for lunch."

"I wanted to surprise her," Jared replied easily, throwing Maggie's companion a challenging glance and catching the look of guilt that flashed in her green eyes.

"We walked to the store to pick up a few groceries," Maggie explained, unaware of the tension. "Oh Jared," Maggie rushed on, "Nicky is such a sweet baby, and so adorable. I bet you're thrilled to have your son and your wife home at last.''

"Thrilled doesn't even begin to describe how I feel." Gritting his teeth, he curved his mouth into what he hoped would pass as a smile.

Faith heard the barely suppressed sarcasm in Jared's voice, and as she met his gaze she could feel the anger coming off him in waves. He was staring at her with an intensity that sent a shiver of apprehension chasing through her.

She knew why he'd rushed home and why he was so angry, but she also sensed something different about him, something she couldn't define.

"When I called this morning to see how you were doing, I was so surprised when Paula answered," Maggie continued brightly. "I insisted on coming over to see the baby. We've had a lovely visit. Haven't we, Paula?" She turned to smile at Faith.

"Yes," Faith acknowledged, dragging her gaze from Jared's. "I hope we can do it again," she added politely.

"Me, too. Well, much as I'd love to stay and chat, I'd better take my son home and feed him his lunch. But listen, now that Paula and the baby are back home, maybe we can all get together one evening."

"That sounds like a great idea," Jared was quick to reply. "How about this weekend?"

"Oh! Well…that would be wonderful." Maggie's tone was hesitant. "But you should check with your wife first," she said. "Having a new baby in the house takes some adjusting to. Believe me, I know.'' She flashed Faith an understanding smile.

Jared turned to Faith. ''What about it, darling?'' he asked. ''Are you feeling up to doing a little entertaining?''

Faith felt her pulse flutter in reaction to Jared's casual endearment. ''Of course,'' she calmly assured him.

''Good.'' Jared immediately turned back to Maggie. ''How does Saturday suit you?''

Maggie's gaze darted to Faith. ''Saturday's fine,'' she replied tentatively. ''But...''

''That's settled,'' Jared declared, as he bent to lift Nicky out of his stroller.

Beside him, Faith kept her smile in place. She had the distinct impression Jared had issued the invitation to see how she would react, but if she'd surprised him with her easy acceptance he didn't show it.

''Great! I'll talk to you tomorrow, Paula,'' Maggie said, and with a wave she moved off.

Faith retrieved the grocery bags from the back of the stroller and followed Jared into the house. Once inside, he immediately turned to face her, his gaze piercing.

''Before you say anything,'' Faith said, quickly jumping in, ''I'm sorry we weren't here—''

''Really!'' Jared interjected, his tone disbelieving.

''I know I shouldn't have gone with Maggie to the store,'' she hurried on. ''But there was no milk, juice or much of anything edible in the fridge, and only two tins of Nicky's formula left. I thought we'd be back in time. I'm sorry,'' she repeated earnestly.

If he'd needed proof this woman wasn't Paula, he'd just been handed it. He couldn't recall Paula ever apologizing for anything. And to hear her apologize, not once but twice in the space of a few minutes, confirmed what he'd begun to suspect as they'd stood outside talking to Maggie.

''You sound like you really mean that,'' Jared responded. As he studied her features more closely, he noticed several subtle differences in her appearance he should have spotted before. Differences he admitted now he'd been too caught up in his own anger to see.

Her hair was slightly longer and a darker shade of brown. Her lips were fuller, more sensuous, and he could see a smattering of freckles on her nose. But more telling by far was the look of sadness lurking in her eyes, a sadness that tugged strangely at his heart.

Hadn't DeMarco said something about Paula's sister losing a baby? Such a tragedy would account for the sorrow he'd seen, and having had a child of her own explained why she'd handled Nicky with such confidence and efficiency.

Jared remembered standing in the doorway of the bedroom in the house in San Francisco watching her change Nicky's diaper and thinking to himself that she seemed an entirely different person altogether. He'd been right.

''I do mean it.'' The words reiterating her apology penetrated Jared's distracted thoughts. Suddenly the realization hit him that this woman who looked so familiar was actually a stranger—and not the mother of his child as he'd believed.

Confusion and anger warred within him, but he stifled the impulse to demand an explanation.

Nicky began to squirm in his arms.

"He's probably hungry, and he definitely needs a diaper change," Jared heard the woman say.

He drew a steadying breath. "I'll do it," he responded, relieved to have an opportunity to have some time alone in order to come to terms with the startling turn of events.

Upstairs, he undressed the baby and proceeded to change his soiled diaper. His thoughts were racing. Why had Paula enlisted the help of her sister? They were up to something, he was sure of it. This bizarre development seemed to confirm his suspicion that she'd changed her mind about giving him sole custody of the baby.

His hands stilled for a moment and a chill ran through him. Gazing down at his infant son, he felt tears sting his eyes at the thought of losing Nicky. A pain the like of which he'd never felt before tore at his heart.

Silently gritting his teeth, he renewed his vow to do everything in his power to keep his son here in Grace Harbor where he could provide him with all the love, stability and security he deserved.

The impulse to confront the woman pretending to be Paula and demand she tell him what they were planning flared to life again. But he reined in his anger, deciding the best course of action was no action at all. He'd simply bide his time and play a waiting game.

Downstairs, Faith busied herself putting away the perishable items while warming a bottle for Nicky. She couldn't blame Jared for being angry, but there had been something disturbing about the way he'd looked at her, almost as if he'd been trying to see inside her soul.

It was obvious Paula's marriage to Jared was rife with problems. Why else would she have run off days before the baby was due? And since her return, he hadn't objected when she'd taken up residence in the spare bedroom, nor had he attempted to reconcile with her. But from what she'd seen of Jared, he cared deeply for his son, and it was entirely possible that behind his anger, he still cared for Paula, the mother of his son.

Faith knew from her own brief but painful experience with marriage that it wasn't always a bed of roses. She could only hope Paula would come to her senses and for the sake of the two most important people in her life, put her own ambitions on hold and salvage her marriage before it deteriorated beyond repair.

"Here we are." Jared's voice sliced through Faith's wayward thoughts. "Nicky must be starving. He's been trying to suck his fist."

"Do you want to feed him?" Faith asked, testing the warmth of the milk on the inside of her wrist.

"I'd love to. But I have to get back to the office," Jared replied, his tone wistful.

"I thought...I mean, aren't you—" Faith broke off, feeling her face grow warm.

"No, I'm not taking him to the office with me, if that's what you're trying to ask. He's had quite enough upheaval these past few days."

Faith swallowed the lump of emotion lodged in her throat. "Thank you," she managed to say as she reached out to take Nicky from him.

Jared relinquished his hold on his son. Though he was still trying to come to terms with the knowledge that this woman wasn't Paula, one thing he was sure of, Nicky's welfare had always been her primary concern.

On reflection he realized that he should have known something was amiss when he'd confronted her outside her house in San Francisco. But he'd been so elated at finding his son he'd railroaded right over her objections.

Leaning forward, Jared dropped a kiss on the top of his son's head. "I'll be back around six."

"We'll be here," Faith assured him, her voice a husky whisper, as the spicy scent of his aftershave swarmed her senses, catapulting her pulse into overdrive.

With a nod, Jared turned and walked away.

Faith drew a ragged breath. For the briefest of seconds she'd had the foolish notion Jared was going to kiss her. But even more outrageous was the ache of disappointment washing over her because he hadn't.

Nicky let out a wail, effectively drawing her attention away from the emotions churning inside her.

After giving her young nephew his bottle, Faith tucked him into his crib and, needing to distract herself, retrieved her sketch pad, charcoal and pencils from her knapsack and ventured outside onto the sundeck.

She stood at the railing and looked down on the neglected garden. A thick carpet of red, gold and rust-colored leaves from the birch and maple trees outlining the property littered the grass below.

Rhododendron bushes, a favorite of Faith's, were scattered around the yard, and Faith wondered what color their blossoms would be come spring.

The sun was already making its slow descent, peeking intermittently from behind a gathering of gray clouds. The October temperature had dipped to the low fifties, adding a crispness to the air that held the promise of winter.

But the chill was soon forgotten as Faith's gaze focused on the panoramic view beyond the garden. Over the tops of the trees she could see an endless row of sand dunes and beyond them, stretching toward the horizon, a silvery wide band of ocean, shimmering and glinting in the fading sunlight.

Faith opened her sketch pad, and soon filled several pages as she recreated the images before her. Oblivious to the cold temperature, she became so absorbed in what she was doing she didn't hear the telephone when it started to ring. The strident noise broke through her concentration and with a panicked gasp she closed her sketch pad and hurried inside.

"Hello?" she said breathlessly.

"Where were you?" Jared's deep resonant voice was tinged with both anger and relief.

"Out on the sundeck."

"Isn't it a little cool for Nicky to be out there?" he asked.

"Nicky's asleep upstairs. I only stepped outside for a few minutes," she added lamely, then, glancing at the clock on the stove, realized she'd been sketching for almost an hour.

She shivered, aware of just how cold she was.

"I called to let you know I've invited two more guests to dinner on Saturday," Jared said.

Faith frowned. "Oh...who?" she asked.

"Stephanie and Dave Perrin," Jared replied. "I ran into them outside my office. You met them during the summer, remember?"

"Ah...yes," Faith lied as her pulse picked up speed. "H-how are they?" she inquired politely.

"Fine. I think it would be best if we kept things simple. If I pick up a fresh salmon at the fish market on Saturday, we could have a barbecue."

"A barbecue?" Faith repeated, shivering anew. "Isn't it a little late in the season to be eating outside?"

"Who said anything about eating outside?" Jared's tone was teasing. "If we barbecue a salmon, throw on a half dozen potatoes to bake, add a tossed salad and finish up with a cheesecake concoction from the bakery in town, dinner would be a snap.''

Faith was silent for a moment. Jared's menu was deliciously simple, yet quietly elegant. ''Sounds great.''

''Good,'' Jared said, and Faith could hear the smile in his voice. ''I'll see you later.''

''Wait!'' Faith quickly jumped in. ''It's only three o'clock. Aren't you going to call and check up on me again in an hour?'' she asked, suddenly wanting to reestablish the old animosity, sensing at some point during the conversation an invisible threshold had been crossed.

''I didn't say I wouldn't be calling,'' Jared replied before quietly hanging up.

Faith replaced the receiver. His call was thoughtful. During her marriage to Glen, he'd thought nothing of bringing home several colleagues for dinner without giving her any warning, expecting her to magically whip up a gourmet feast and serve it on a table decorated in a style fit for a king.

But what she found most endearing was that Jared had actually planned the dinner menu, a menu requiring a minimum of work on her part. His gesture revealed a considerate man, one obviously willing to pitch in. One maybe even willing to forgive and forget past mistakes.

Faith felt a hand squeeze her heart. Paula was lucky to have found a man like Jared, and again Faith hoped her twin would come to her senses. Not that Faith had anything against women pursuing careers. After all, she'd had a career of her own during her marriage to Glen. But if Paula succeeded in breaking into show business, her high-profile career would be much more demanding, leaving little time for her husband and son.

Faith had to believe Paula would ultimately make the right choice, if only for Nicky's sake.

When Jared walked through from the garage around six o'clock, he was greeted with the delicious scent of chicken cooking in tarragon.

Glancing down at the brown paper bag in his hand, he shoved it in the closet along with his coat. He'd assumed Paula's twin would be like her sister in every respect. That's why he'd stopped on his way home to pick up a take-out dinner from one of the restaurants on Main Street.

He'd spent the afternoon trying to reduce the pile of paperwork on his desk, paperwork he'd neglected during the past two weeks. But his mind hadn't been on the files—they'd been on Faith Nelson, Paula's sister, the woman caring for his son.

He'd upbraided himself a thousand times for not realizing at the outset she wasn't Paula, and on thinking back to that first encounter, he realized she'd tried to tell him he'd made a mistake. What should have tipped him off was seeing the loving, caring way she'd tended to Nicky. And the way she'd challenged him about driving without a proper car seat. She'd acted like a tiger protecting her cub.

More than a little baffled by her outburst, he'd found himself admiring the way she'd stood up to him, especially for a cause as important as Nicky's safety.

But while a part of him had applauded the changes he'd seen in Paula, he'd deliberately chosen to ignore them. He'd been afraid to acknowledge that his carefully drawn-up plans might well be in serious jeopardy.

The sound of water running and a cupboard being closed brought his musings to an end. He headed for the kitchen, coming to a halt in the doorway.

Faith stood at the sink with her back to him. Jared let his gaze drift over her, assessing and comparing. Although she looked remarkably like Paula, Faith had demonstrated none of the selfishness or superficiality inherent in her twin.

In Faith he'd seen only a genuine warmth as well as sincerity in everything she'd done. He'd been forced to place his trust in her, and she'd proved herself up to the test, leaving him to wonder how he could ever have mistaken her for Paula.

But they were twins, he quickly reminded himself, and twins were known to share a close bond. They'd collaborated in a scheme to deceive him, and for the sake of his son, Jared knew he couldn't afford to lower his guard.

Faith turned from the sink, and Jared heard her startled gasp at finding him there.

"I didn't hear you come in," she said, her smile tentative.

"What's for dinner? Something smells wonderful,'' Jared said, noticing the hint of pink on her cheeks and the pulse jumping at her throat. ''Is Nicky in bed?''

''Yes,'' Faith answered, noting the flash of disappointment that came into his eyes. ''But he's due to wake up shortly. Dinner's almost ready,'' she went on, wishing she knew whether Jared liked to eat right away or preferred to unwind first by changing into something more casual.

''Can I help with anything?''

''Thanks, but everything is under control,'' Faith assured him, warmed by his offer. Glen had rarely if ever raised a finger to help around the house.

''Do I have time to pop upstairs and change?''

''Of course,'' Faith replied, flashing a nervous smile. ''Check on Nicky while you're up there,'' she suggested.

He grinned. ''I'll make it my first stop.''

Jared rejoined her in the kitchen ten minutes later. Seeing him dressed in a pair of faded blue jeans and a white T-shirt, looking decidedly approachable and stunningly attractive, Faith felt her pulse pick up speed.

''Nicky's still asleep,'' he told her as he approached the table and pulled out a chair.

''Let's hope we'll be finished eating before he wakes up,'' Faith commented, and began spooning a piece of steaming hot tarragon chicken onto a plate.

''Thanks.'' Jared accepted the plate she handed him.

Faith served herself and sat down across from him. "You…ah, we're lucky Nicky's such a happy and contented baby," she said, attempting to make conversation. "He's not like—" She broke off abruptly, guiltily darting a glance across the table as she felt a blush warm her cheeks.

"Nicky's not like who?" Jared asked with a frown.

"Would you care for salad?" Faith asked, pushing the bowl toward him. "Oh…just a minute, I forgot the dressing." She leapt to her feet and crossed to the fridge, hoping once she returned to the table, Jared wouldn't pursue the question. She'd blundered again. She'd been about to say Nicky wasn't at all like Erica.

"Thanks," Jared said as she set the bottle of salad dressing in front of him. "Who is Nicky not like?"

Her cheeks grew warm. "Oh…he's not like some babies who suffer from colic and cry a lot. I read about it somewhere," she added with a calmness she was far from feeling.

Resuming her seat, she pretended an interest in the food on her plate, aware of Jared's steady gaze on her.

"Was it in one of those books on child rearing I brought home?"

Faith kept her gaze averted and lied. "Yes," she replied, intrigued by the notion Jared had taken an interest in the subject.

"I read a few of them. But not one came close to describing the feeling I get every time I look at

Nicky," he quietly confessed. "I still can't believe I have a son, that he's mine...." His voice, filled with awe and pride, trailed off.

Tears suddenly stung her eyes at the sincerity echoing through his words. If she'd had any doubts about Jared's feelings toward Nicky they vanished forever. His love for Nicky was both powerful and intense. Faith felt more than a little envious of Paula, who'd been fortunate to marry a man so deeply committed to family.

For the remainder of the week the days fell into something of a pattern, a pattern governed for the most part by Nicky's feeding and sleeping schedule.

Jared insisted he take his turn of night feedings, though. Nicky was already beginning to sleep through. Each evening when he came home from work he'd bathe and feed Nicky and put him to bed, spending quality time with his son.

Faith was relieved and pleased when Jared stopped calling home to check on her. Instead he'd call only occasionally, and then to ask if she needed anything from the store. His solicitousness toward her and the baby served to enhance her growing admiration of this man who was her sister's husband.

The past four days had been close to idyllic, and Faith acknowledged that the time spent looking after Nicky had gone a long way toward healing the wound left by the loss of her own baby.

But with each passing day Faith became firmly

enmeshed in the role of being Nicky's mother. Even though she kept reminding herself that the situation was only temporary, a part of her wished the dream life she was living would never end.

Chapter Seven

When Saturday morning dawned Faith woke with a feeling of happiness and contentment she'd never thought she'd feel again. Downstairs she found Jared already in the kitchen cooking breakfast.

His warm smile of greeting sent her heart into a tailspin as she watched him serve up a plate of steaming pancakes and coffee. Upstairs Nicky started to cry, but before she could move, Jared put his hand on her shoulder. "I'll take care of him. Enjoy your breakfast," he added before striding toward the stairs.

Faith sat sipping coffee, silently marveling at a man so eager to share his parental responsibilities, and so determined to play a major role in his son's life.

Several hours later, Jared reappeared in the kitchen after taking Nicky upstairs for a nap. "It's almost two o'clock. I'd better get going. I'll pick up the salmon from the market on my way home,'' he added.

"Is Nicky asleep?"

"Yes. But it took a while. He was more interested in watching the mobile above his crib."

Faith smiled. "He's beginning to see the shapes and movements of the animals now."

"And he's starting to smile more often, too," Jared said, warmth and love in his voice.

"Yes, he is." Nicky was awake for longer periods during the day, and he'd started responding to all kinds of stimuli.

"Is there anything we've forgotten?" he asked, capturing her attention.

"Ah...all I can think of is a couple of lemons. I meant to buy them yesterday, but I forgot. Otherwise, I think everything is under control."

"Good. I'm really looking forward to tonight. It's been ages since we...ah, had company for dinner."

In fact, Jared knew it was the first time he'd had anyone in for dinner since moving into the house a year ago. Paula had made no effort to socialize with his friends, repeatedly reminding him there wasn't much point, not when she wouldn't be staying.

But this woman wasn't Paula. If he'd learned anything during the past few days it was how dramatically different in personality and character twins could actually be.

Faith wasn't at all like her sister; in fact, he'd

have to say they were complete opposites. He'd found himself drawn more and more to Faith—her warmth, her smile and particularly her devotion to Nicky.

"I'm looking forward to tonight, too," he heard Faith say, and at her words he smiled. He'd been smiling a lot lately, due, he knew, to the fact that for the first time in his life he was experiencing what being a family was all about, and he didn't want it to end.

"I have to drop in to the office for a while, but I should be back around four," he said. "Everyone's coming at five, aren't they?"

"Yes," Faith replied, ignoring the sudden and erratic pounding of her heart, caused she knew by the smile still curving Jared's mouth, accentuating the cleft in his chin.

For the next hour Faith busied herself tidying the kitchen and setting the dining-room table in readiness for their guests. She'd just put the finishing touches on the table when the phone rang. Thinking the caller might be Jared, she hurried to the kitchen and grabbed the receiver.

"Hello!" she said cheerfully.

"Faith, is that you?"

"Paula! Yes, it's me," Faith replied, the brightness gradually fading from her voice.

"You won't believe what's happened! I've got incredible news," Paula rushed on excitedly. "My agent just called. I got the part! I'm going to be working in a new movie with two of Hollywood's leading actors.'' She followed her announcement with a squeal of pleasure before hurrying on. ''I'm thrilled, flabbergasted, ecstatic! This is the break I've been waiting for…dreaming about. After this, I just know my career is going to skyrocket!''

''Paula! How wonderful! Congratulations,'' Faith said, trying to inject enthusiasm into her voice, all the while thinking Paula seemed to have forgotten Jared's threat to take Nicky away from her.

''I knew this would happen,'' Paula continued, oblivious to Faith's growing concern. ''I'm on cloud nine! I have goose bumps just talking about it! Picture this! My name up on the screen next to theirs!''

''That does sound exciting. But I thought…''

''Filming doesn't start till December, which is great. That gives me lots of time to get back in shape.''

''Paula, wait, aren't you forgetting something? Didn't you get in touch with a lawyer?''

''Why do I need a lawyer? I have a terrific agent, and she's negotiated a great deal.''

''I'm talking about Nicky. You told me Jared threatened to take him away from you if you went back to acting. Have you talked to a lawyer? Maybe if you sat down with your husband and told him your news, explained to Jared just how much—''

''Husband? Did you say husband?'' Paula asked, amusement lacing her voice.

''Yes,'' Faith answered, bewildered by the question.

Laughter echoed down the phone line. "Jared isn't my husband. We're not married."

"Not married!" Faith repeated, reeling from the impact of her sister's astonishing revelation. "But he wears a wedding ring."

"That's just his class ring," Paula explained. "I teasingly told him he should put it on his left hand and I would wear one, too. That way everyone would assume we'd secretly gotten married. It was just a joke!" Paula was laughing.

"You and Jared aren't married?" Faith asked again, wanting to be sure she wasn't mistaken.

"Don't get me wrong. Jared is a nice guy. We had some good times together. But he's one of those guys with old-fashioned ideas about love and marriage, and when he proposed I just told him I wasn't ready for all that. I'll probably never be ready for it.

"Besides, I knew about this project. I'd already read the script, and there was a perfect part in it for me. I couldn't just walk away from my dream, could I?"

Faith couldn't think of a thing to say. Her mind was still mulling over the fact that Jared had offered to marry Paula, had offered to do the honorable thing, and had been turned down.

"What about those threats you told me Jared made?" Faith suddenly asked as she tried to sort things out in her head.

"That's not important right now." Paula brushed aside the question.

"You can't be serious!" Faith protested, astonished by her twin's lack of concern. It didn't make sense...nothing made sense. Unless... Faith's thoughts shuddered to a halt.

"You lied to me about Jared, didn't you?" Faith asked.

"Not exactly," Paula hedged. "He does want custody of Nicky—"

"Why did you lie? Why did you want me to pretend to be you?" Faith interrupted, anger rising like a hot-air balloon inside her. "And while you're at it, maybe you could explain why you ran off in the first place. It's a question Jared has asked a number of times. I'm a little curious to know the answer myself."

Paula made no reply. Several seconds ticked by, and Faith began to wonder if the connection had been broken.

"I'm listening," Faith prompted.

"Look, sis. When you told me Jared had showed up at your house, I couldn't see the harm in letting him go on thinking he'd found me. And I felt better knowing you'd be taking care of Nicky, that's all.

"And the reason I left before Nicky was born was because I felt like a prisoner. Jared was constantly talking about the baby coming and...well, I was tired of the whole deal. He didn't care about me, he only cared about the baby." Paula's tone bordered on petulant.

"So you decided you'd had enough and you were leaving," Faith said.

"Not exactly," Paula repled. "I got an urgent call from my agent telling me the studio had already begun auditioning.

"The auditions weren't supposed to start for another month. I freaked out! I had to do something! I thought if I showed up at the studio, I could somehow convince the casting director that I really was the best candidate," Paula said.

"I knew if I told Jared what I was planning to do he'd stop me. So after he went to work the next morning, I just left. It was stupid, I know," Paula acknowledged. "I guess I could have called him after Nicky was born. But I was afraid that if he came and took the baby, he'd never let me see my son again. And to top it all, I didn't even get to the studio. I went into labor an hour after I arrived in L.A. But right after I gave birth to Nicky, I called my agent and told her I'd be able to make the auditions after all. Lucky for me she'd already managed to push my audition back two weeks."

Faith sighed, having difficulty understanding why her twin had jeopardized the safety of her unborn child simply for the sake of an audition.

It appeared she'd lied about Jared making a threat, and in doing so had involved Faith in an unnecessary deception. A deception that had nothing to do with Nicky's welfare, and everything to do with Paula's own driving ambition to succeed.

"Faith...listen. None of this matters now," Paula said. "Can't you just be happy for me? Don't you understand what getting this part means to me?"

"No, I don't," Faith replied, unable to fathom her twin's total lack of regard for her son's welfare, or for that matter the pain and anguish she'd put Jared through.

"You've never understood." Paula's tone was bitter. "I deserve this chance. I've worked hard for it and nothing is going to stop me."

Faith bit back a sigh. "You still haven't told me what you're going to do about Nicky. Don't you think it's time you got together with Jared and discussed what arrangements you need to make for the baby?"

"All right! All right!" Paula responded, her tone sharp, her annoyance evident.

"It's just that you seem to have forgotten you have a son," Faith said. "Oh, by the way, have you told Mother and Dad about their new grandson yet?" she asked, attempting to change the subject and lighten the conversation a little.

"Not yet. They're on their way to New Zealand to visit Aunt Ruby, remember. And they said they'd be stopping off in Hawaii for a week first."

"You're right. I forgot," Faith said. Their parents had planned to spend several months with her mother's sister, who was recovering from a recent heart operation.

"Look, I've got to go," Paula said, cutting through Faith's drifting thoughts. "I'm meeting my agent and a couple of friends tonight for a drink. At least there's someone around here willing to help me celebrate," she added on a sour note.

"Paula, wait! I am happy for you, really I am, but it's time you faced your responsibilities. Jared is a wonderful father, and he loves Nicky very much. You should meet with Jared, discuss what you think is best for Nicky and make a decision together."

"I suppose you're right," Paula agreed grudgingly. "I'll call the airlines and book a flight to Seattle. I'll be there tomorrow night," she said. "Is that all right with you, sister dear?" Sarcasm gave an edge to Paula's voice. "Or would you rather I abandoned my celebrations and get on a plane tonight?"

Faith stifled another sigh. "Tomorrow will be fine," she said calmly. "And Paula, congrat—" Faith began, but her sister had already hung up.

When Faith replaced the receiver she could hear Nicky crying upstairs. Muttering under her breath, she headed to the nursery.

Half an hour later, Faith was still in the nursery when she heard a noise from downstairs telling her Jared had returned.

Faith felt her heartbeat accelerate. For the first time since he'd walked into her life a week ago she suddenly felt shy and uncertain about seeing him.

Ever since Paula had laughingly announced that Jared wasn't her husband, Faith had been wrestling with this news, telling herself it changed nothing, yet knowing in a private corner of her heart that she was only fooling herself.

Faith rewound the music box mobile suspended

over Nicky's crib before slipping across the hall to her bedroom. She felt sure Jared would peek in on his son, and she wasn't ready to face him.

Regardless of this latest development, Nicky's welfare was still Faith's primary concern, and it saddened her that Nicky wasn't a major priority in Paula's life. During the entire telephone conversation, Paula hadn't once asked how Nicky was doing, if he was all right, if he was happy. Faith felt deeply ashamed and more than a little angry at her twin. Didn't Paula realize how truly blessed she was?

It seemed ironic that Paula had found a man as wonderful as Jared, a man willing to accept responsibility for his actions, a man deeply committed to raising his son, giving him the love and attention he deserved. Instead of embracing the miracle she'd been given, instead of joyfully accepting the wonderful gift, Paula had abandoned her family, for a chance to be in the spotlight.

And while Faith acknowledged it was probably too late, she vowed for Nicky's sake to try once more to make her sister see just what she was throwing away.

What about Jared? During the past few days his anger at her, or at Paula rather, had for all intents and purposes vanished. They'd actually been enjoying a kind of harmony. Faith found herself wondering if Jared was beginning to think Paula had changed her mind and was content in her role as a mother.

Suddenly the prospect of continuing the deception

one more day weighed heavily on her shoulders. Was it really fair, now that Paula was coming to Grace Harbor, to keep Jared in the dark?

An hour ago she'd been looking forward to the evening ahead, but now she was preoccupied with the question of whether or not she should tell Jared the truth.

What would he think of her? How would he react when he found out she wasn't Paula? He would have every reason to hate her, and every reason to throw her out.

It was with a heavy heart that Faith ventured from the relative sanctuary of her room. Having brought only jeans and a few sweaters with her, she'd been forced into choosing one of Paula's dresses from the closet. She'd settled on a navy dress with long sleeves. Its silky texture gently hugged her curves, while its flared skirt reached her knees. She felt overdressed and self-conscious, but she really had no choice.

Brushing her hair till it shone, she used two tortoiseshell combs to secure it away from her face. In an attempt to boost her confidence she'd applied a minimum amount of makeup to highlight her lips and cheekbones.

Jared finished seasoning the salmon using a mixture of herbs and spices, and was wrapping it in foil in readiness for the barbecue when he heard Faith coming downstairs. He hadn't seen her since his return and had assumed she was in her bedroom getting ready for the dinner party.

Reaching for the towel nearby, he dried his hands and glanced up in time to see her enter the kitchen. The sight of Faith wearing one of Paula's dresses, looking like a model in a fashion magazine, sent his pulse racing and his heart spinning out of control.

She looked incredibly beautiful. But unlike Paula's superficial beauty, Faith's came from within, from the warm, wonderful, caring way she gave of herself.

"You look fabulous." Jared spoke softly, and smiled as a rush of color suffused her face at his compliment.

She gazed down at her hands, twisting them in a nervous gesture that tugged at his heart. "Thank you," she responded in a breathless tone, making him want to haul her into his arms and ravage her trembling mouth.

One thing he knew—whoever Faith's ex-husband had been, the man was a fool.

"Everything's ready to go on the barbecue," Jared said as he took a step toward her. "The table looks terrific, by the way."

"Thank you," Faith mumbled. Keeping her eyes averted, she moved behind the kitchen table, shying away from him like a high-strung filly.

Jared wasn't altogether surprised she was nervous about the evening ahead. After all, unlike Paula, she'd never met Stephanie and Dave, or Dylan, before. But when she continued to avoid making eye contact with him, he suddenly had the strong impression there was more to her reaction than simply nervousness. "Is Nicky due to be fed soon?"

Faith glanced at the clock on the stove. "He'll probably wake up when everyone arrives."

"Good! I like a kid with good timing. That way I won't have to wake him up to show him off," he added, but there was no answering smile from Faith.

Puzzled, Jared tossed the towel onto the counter. "Paula? Is everything all right?"

"Yes! Of course!" she replied brightly, too brightly.

Jared heard the tremor in her voice, and noted the flash of guilt in her green eyes.

Something was definitely wrong! He could feel it. What could have happened to cause this change in her?

A thought struck him. Could Paula have called while he was out? It was a logical explanation for Faith's unusual behavior and one that put him on immediate alert.

"I'm just a little nervous about tonight," Jared heard her say.

"Don't be," he responded, his tone reassuring, but all the while his thoughts were racing. He was tempted to ask her outright whether Paula had called, but a quick glance at the clock told him there wasn't enough time, not with guests arriving in less than half an hour. "I'd better hit the shower. I'll be down in fifteen minutes."

Jared took the stairs two at a time. Earlier at the

office when he'd replayed the messages on his answering machine there had been a call from Greg Dunsford.

Greg hadn't had much to report. He'd told Jared about the audition Paula had attended the previous day, but for the most part, Paula had been staying close to the hotel, spending her time in her room or in the hotel gym.

Had Paula decided on her next move? Jared wondered. Had she called Faith to tell her what the next phase of her plan was going to be?

Jared stood under the hot spray of the shower trying to think of a way to stop Paula. Faith was the key. Somehow he had to get her to tell him what they were planning. But how?

Shutting off the shower, he stepped out onto the mat and reached for the towel hanging on the rail. After drying himself, he wiped the steam from the bathroom mirror.

Jared lathered the lower half of his face, then picked up the razor. He stopped to stare at his reflection. He'd often overheard women comment on his good looks, but he could see nothing out of the ordinary in his appearance.

An old girlfriend had once accused him of being too good-looking, of having too much charm. Did he have enough charm to entice a woman to share her innermost secrets?

Jared smiled. Maybe it was time to put this so-called charm of his to the test.

From the moment the doorbell rang announcing Maggie and Dylan's arrival, followed a few minutes later by Stephanie and Dave, Faith knew the evening would be a success.

As she'd predicted, Nicky woke soon after their guests arrived, and when Jared brought his son downstairs, his face beamed with pride as he accepted congratulations from his friends.

Maggie and Stephanie took turns feeding Nicky his bottle. Faith shooed the men out onto the sundeck, where they cooked dinner and argued over the prospect of Nicky and Dylan junior becoming hockey or basketball players.

Faith put Nicky to bed around seven, and it wasn't long before they were all seated at the dining-room table enjoying the delicious barbecued salmon.

Conversation flowed easily during the meal, and while Faith was careful to keep her contribution to a minimum, she soon got over her nervousness, silently acknowledging that Jared's friends were warm, wonderful people.

She especially noticed the chemistry between Maggie and her husband, Dylan, their shared smiles and secret glances.

While the women cleared away the dishes, the men wandered through to the living room, and it was then Faith asked Maggie how she and Dylan had met.

Maggie related an extraordinary tale, confessing

to having had a crush on Dylan, a lieutenant commander in the U.S. Navy and favorite nephew of her father's new wife, from the first moment she set eyes on him.

When her father and Dylan's aunt perished in a plane crash, Dylan had come to Grace Harbor to attend the funeral. During that highly emotional and heartbreaking weekend, he and Maggie had made love.

The next day Dylan had been called back to his base, and as he neared San Diego he'd been involved in a car accident, resulting in a total loss of his memory.

Nearly nine months after the accident, Dylan, following the only lead he had to his past, a letter he'd received from Jared regarding his aunt's will, had returned to Grace Harbor in the hope of jarring his memory.

He'd come face-to-face with Maggie, pregnant with his child, but he hadn't recognized her. Through the strength of her love for him and the birth of their child, Dylan had eventually recovered his memory, and they'd found each other again.

After hearing Maggie's wonderfully romantic story, Faith found her thoughts turning to Jared. All evening she'd had the feeling he might be seeking to reconcile with Paula, to put their relationship on a more intimate level.

He'd been more attentive than usual, more considerate, drawing her into conversations, gently teasing her and finding excuses to touch her. Faith tried to tell herself it was all for the benefit of their guests.

But when they rejoined the men in the living room Jared instantly rose from the easy chair, to cross to her side. When she felt his arm go around her to pull her against his muscular frame, in a loverlike gesture, her legs threatened to give way.

For the next hour as they sat chatting to their guests, Faith grew increasingly aware of Jared's slow yet deliberate seduction.

Sitting next to him on the love seat, she could feel the pressure of his thigh against hers, a pressure that sent the blood humming through her veins.

And when his fingers deliberately skimmed her shoulder, and his breath fanned her cheek as he leaned over to make a point, she was aware only of the ripple of desire that chased through her, making her weak with longing.

Jared's smile told her he knew exactly what he was doing, and the effect he was having on her. And the fact that this subtle but deliberate seduction was taking place in full view of his friends made it impossible for Faith to do anything to stop him.

"It's been a lovely evening," Maggie said some ten minutes later. "But I think it's time I took my husband home. We don't want to be too late for the baby-sitter. Otherwise she might not sit for us again."

"We'd better hit the road, too," Dave said, rising from the easy chair.

"Thanks for a great dinner. The company wasn't bad either," Dylan quipped, giving Jared's arm a friendly punch.

"It'll be your turn next time," Jared countered.

"Deal," Dylan replied, then turned to Faith. "Thanks, Paula, for everything. I have a feeling your husband is anxious to have you to himself," he teased gently, sending the blood rushing to her cheeks.

"You got that right," Jared answered softly. Putting his arm around Faith, he drew her against him, dropping a featherlight kiss on her mouth.

Dizzy from the sensations suddenly spiraling through her, Faith had little memory of the next ten minutes. All she was aware of was Jared's arm around her, of his body pressed against hers, of the tingling warmth lingering on her lips and of the desire slowly building inside her.

The sound of Jared closing the front door brought her out of her daze. Her first instinct was to escape, to run for the sanctuary of her room, because though it broke her heart to admit it, Paula was the one Jared thought he was seducing. Paula was the one he wanted.

Before she could take even one step, Jared turned her to face him.

"I think we both need this, don't you?" he said.

Any protest she might have made was forgotten as his mouth claimed hers in a kiss that robbed her of breath, and stole her heart away.

The world careened out of control, and all Faith could do was hang on for the ride. Exciting! Electrifying! Erotic! That was the only way to describe what was happening. Nothing in her life had prepared her for this, and she never wanted the kiss to end.

It seemed so outrageous, impossible in fact, that one dynamic kiss could catapult her so swiftly to the edge of reason.

She wanted Jared. Wanted him with an intensity that shocked her. And it was obvious he wanted her, too.

No. The denial came from somewhere inside her head as she remembered she wasn't the woman he wanted at all.... He thought she was Paula!

Pain sliced through Faith, and somehow she found the strength to pull away.

"Jared, please stop!" she said, her breathing ragged.

"Why?" Jared's voice was a hoarse whisper of need.

"You don't understand," she went on, struggling to break free of his embrace. "I'm not Paula! I'm her twin sister, Faith," she blurted out. Drawing a steadying breath, she braced herself for his anger and outrage.

Her words were met with silence.

"Did you hear what I said?" she asked, puzzled by his lack of response.

"I heard you," Jared replied on a sigh as he released her. "I know who you are," he told her. "I've known it for a while. Now tell me something I don't know. You heard from Paula today, didn't you? What is she up to? She's planning to steal Nicky away from me, isn't she?"

Chapter Eight

Faith staggered back, stunned by Jared's revelation.

"You know I'm not Paula?"

"Yes, I know you're not Paula. You're Faith Nelson, her twin sister."

Faith blinked. "But, how…?"

Jared quickly explained how he'd learned the truth. As Faith listened, she wasn't sure whether she was relieved or angry that he'd known her identity for some time.

"Let's continue this conversation in the living room, shall we?" he suggested. "I don't know about you, but I could use a drink."

As Jared ushered her into the room, Faith tried to gather her scattered thoughts. In a matter of hours she'd gone from being soundly kissed by a man she'd grown to admire during the past few days, a man she believed was married to her sister, to learning he wasn't married to Paula after all and he'd known almost from the outset she'd been impersonating her twin.

"Brandy?" Jared asked as he crossed to the coffee table containing the tray of liqueurs.

"No, thank you." Faith dropped into the easy chair.

Jared poured himself a brandy, and after taking a generous sip moved to stand in front of the fireplace.

"Paula called this afternoon while I was out, didn't she?" he repeated.

Startled, Faith glanced up to find Jared staring at her intently. "Yes." There was little point lying.

"What's she up to? What scheme is she planning next?" Frustration and anger colored his tone. "If she thinks I'm going to stand by and let her take my son without a fight, she's mad."

"She is Nicky's mother. She loves him," she protested. But her voice lacked conviction, and even as she spoke the words she wasn't sure she actually believed them.

Jared snorted. "You don't believe that any more than I do. Paula loves Paula, period, and she isn't any more interested in raising her son than in taking up swimming lessons. She's only interested in using him, or you, or anyone for that matter as long as she ends up getting what she wants."

Faith's breath caught in her throat. Jared's analysis of Paula was decidedly astute.

"I'm right, aren't I?" he challenged.

"Don't you think you're painting rather a harsh

picture of her? Paula is ambitious, and yes, she is selfish at times, but that's human nature. We're all guilty of selfishness now and then," she defended. "Besides, you must have seen something appealing about her," she added bluntly, and watched as color crept up his neck and face.

"Point taken," he acknowledged. "But from the moment she told me she was pregnant, I knew she had her own game plan. And I was right." He downed the remainder of the brandy.

"Jared—"

"She didn't want Nicky," he interrupted, his tone brutal. "She signed a paper granting me sole custody of the baby. Everything was going according to plan until she ran off.

"All I could think of was she'd suddenly had a change of heart. But I'm beginning to wonder if she even has a heart," he added bitterly. "If it takes everything I have, I'm prepared to fight to keep my son right here with me where he belongs."

Faith heard the fierce determination in Jared's voice, as well as the fear lurking just beneath the surface. She hadn't until now realized how deeply he loved Nicky, and she was hard-pressed to offer up any argument.

"All I know is Paula said she'd be here sometime tomorrow. She wants to talk to you, to try and sort things out," Faith told him, wishing she could offer Jared some reassurance.

"And you believed her?" Jarred scoffed.

Faith flinched. She kept telling herself he had

every right to be furious with her, every right to think she wasn't telling the truth.

"If you want me to leave, I'll understand," she said, and rose from the chair.

Jared darted her a startled glance, and for a moment Faith glimpsed an emotion in the depths of his eyes he quickly masked. "What's the point?" he countered.

"I should have told you who I was from the start. I'm truly sorry."

"You may have been living a lie," Jared said, "but for what it's worth, I believe you were only doing it for Nicky's sake. I doubt he'd be such a happy, contented baby if you hadn't been here to take care of him. For that I thank you."

Faith felt a warmth spread through her at his words. Looking after Nicky had been both a joy and a comfort. Paula's arrival tomorrow would change everything.

"It's late, and I'm rather tired," Faith said, suddenly weary.

Jared made no move to detain her. Once upstairs, she peeked in on Nicky, who was sleeping soundly. She stood staring down at the child who'd come to mean everything to her, and felt her eyes sting with tears.

She knew it would break her heart to leave Nicky. Taking care of a healthy, happy baby had proved to be a cathartic experience, allowing her to finally come to terms with the loss of her daughter.

But it wasn't only the thought of leaving Nicky

that brought an ache to her heart. In one short week, she'd grown to care for the man who was Nicky's father. He'd shown her there were still honorable, sensitive and caring men left in the world; men willing to accept their responsibilities; men capable of loving a child, completely and unconditionally.

Faith sat up in bed with a start, wondering what had awakened her. Glancing at the clock on her bedside table, she saw it was a little after six. The chimes of the doorbell suddenly echoed through the house.

Pushing the covers aside, she grabbed her sweater from the foot of the bed. She opened her bedroom door in time to see Jared, wearing only his jeans, hurrying down the hallway.

"Who the blazes can that be at this hour?" he mumbled as he disappeared downstairs.

Faith came to a halt at the top of the stairs, wondering if Paula was their early-morning visitor.

"Sheriff Yates! Good morning. Is there a problem?" she heard Jared ask.

"I'm sorry to disturb you, Mr. McAndrew," came the reply. "But it's very important. Do you know a Ms. Paula Preston?"

"Yes," Jared replied cautiously.

"Your name and address were found amongst Ms. Preston's belongings. Are you, by any chance, a relative?"

"In a manner of speaking," Jared hedged.

"Why?" he asked before darting a glance toward the stairs.

"Would you happen to know how we could get in touch with Ms. Preston's family?" Sheriff Yates continued.

"You'd better come in." Jared stood aside. Closing the outer door, he turned to see Faith making her way down the stairs, an anxious expression on her face. "Sheriff Yates, this is Faith Nelson. She's Paula's twin sister," Jared explained.

The sheriff removed his hat. Holding it against his chest, he nodded solemnly. "Ms. Nelson."

"Sheriff, what is it? What's happened?" Faith asked, sensing from the somber look on the man's face that something was dreadfully wrong.

"There's been an accident."

"An accident? My sister? Is she all right?" Faith took a step toward the sheriff.

Sheriff Yates met her gaze and slowly shook his head. "I'm sorry to have to tell you, miss, but your sister is dead."

Faith gasped and took a step back. "No! There's been a mistake." She darted a frightened glance at Jared. "I talked to her yesterday. She was fine. She's coming here today. Please, there must be some mistake," Faith repeated, as if saying the words would somehow make them true.

Jared crossed to where Faith stood shivering, her face ashen, her expression a mixture of shock and disbelief. Putting his arm around her, he urged her to lean on him.

"Sheriff Yates," Jared said, turning to the officer. "Could you tell us what happened? Was it a car accident?"

"No," the sheriff replied. "A call came through to my office a little while ago from a patrolman in L.A. Apparently Ms. Preston had been celebrating with a few friends last night. They'd been drinking in the hotel bar and had moved outside to the hotel grounds, where they started creating quite a disturbance.

"Several hotel guests called the front desk to complain, and the police were called in. When the two patrolmen got there, Ms. Preston, whom they described to be in a highly intoxicated state, had climbed up one of the large concrete fountains in the garden."

"What happened?" Jared asked, urgency in his voice.

"According to witnesses, she turned to wave to her friends and lost her footing. She fell, hitting her head on the concrete. She was pronounced dead at the scene."

"No! No...!" Faith sagged against Jared. She could imagine Paula behaving foolishly, but to risk her life!

"I'm sorry for your loss, miss," the sheriff said, but Faith was too shocked to answer.

"Thank you, Sheriff." Jared tightened his hold on Faith.

At that moment Nicky started crying. Faith automatically turned toward the sound.

"Why don't you go upstairs and take care of Nicky," Jared suggested. "I'll be up in a minute, once I see the sheriff out."

Faith drew a steadying breath, blinking back the tears gathering in her eyes. "All right." Moving out of the shelter of his arms, she turned and climbed the stairs.

Up in the nursery, Faith deliberately pushed all thoughts of Paula from her mind.

Lifting Nicky from the crib, she held him against her breast and murmured soft words of comfort. Crossing to the rocking chair, she sat down, wondering for a moment if the reason Nicky had awakened was that he'd somehow sensed the horrible tragedy that had befallen his mother.

It couldn't be true! Paula wasn't dead! It had to be a mistake! But while her brain tried desperately to deny it, she knew in her heart it was true.

Drawing a deep, ragged breath, Faith fought to keep the pain and sorrow threatening to swamp her at bay.

Though their relationship hadn't been as close as some twins enjoyed, the realization that she would never again see her beautiful, talented sister, that Paula's dreams of stardom were lost forever, evoked a deep and profound sadness.

"Is Nicky all right?" Jared's softly spoken question cut through her musings. Unable to speak, Faith simply nodded. "Should I warm a bottle for him?" he asked.

This time Faith shook her head. Tears were gathering in her eyes, but she blinked them away, fearful that once she started to cry, she might never stop.

Nicky had fallen back to sleep, but Faith was reluctant to relinquish her hold on him. She lingered for a few moments more, then rising from the chair, she returned Nicky to the comfort of his crib.

After covering him with his blanket, she stood staring down at her sister's child. She found a small measure of comfort in the knowledge that Paula's spirit would live on in Nicky, that she'd left behind a wonderful legacy.

When she turned to leave she was surprised to see Jared standing in the doorway. He took a step toward her.

"Faith, I'm so sorry." His voice was a whisper of sound. "I know Paula and I were at odds about Nicky, but she was his mother and she didn't deserve such a horrible fate."

Faith heard the pain and sincerity in his voice, and suddenly it was all too much as the block of emotion lodged in her throat broke free in a heart-wrenching sob.

Jared reacted instantly, pulling her against his solid frame, and as his arms closed around her, a torrent of tears poured down her cheeks.

He held her to him while she wept tears of anger, of regret and of sorrow, until, exhausted, she could weep no more.

When Jared lifted her into his arms and carried her to her bedroom, she didn't have the strength to either protest or resist. And as she drifted off to sleep, she thought she felt his mouth, as soft as an angel's, briefly brush hers.

It had been two weeks since Paula's death. Faith was sitting in the nursery trying to get her cranky nephew to go to sleep.

"Is that my son I hear whining and crying?" Jared said as he entered the nursery. "Why don't you let me try to settle him down," he offered.

"He's all yours," Faith responded with some relief, rising from the rocking chair. "He's been fussing all day. He doesn't have a temperature, but I'm wondering if he's coming down with a cold or something."

"I hope not," Jared said, deftly taking his son from Faith. In slow circular motions he began rubbing Nicky's back and was instantly rewarded with a noisy burp.

"Atta boy! I bet you feel better," Jared added with a chuckle.

Faith smiled. "You certainly have a knack with him."

"Thanks, I think. Oh, Faith."

She turned and met his gaze, feeling her heart jam against her rib cage in reaction.

"We need to talk," he said.

Faith nodded. "I'll be in the kitchen," she said before slipping from the room.

Downstairs, she busied herself making a pot of tea. While she waited for the water to boil her thoughts drifted over the past two weeks. Jared had been a tower of strength, insisting on being the one to fly to L.A. Faith had offered little opposition, agreeing with Jared's argument that it would simplify matters if she stayed and took care of Nicky.

Difficult as it had been, they'd discussed funeral arrangements. She'd agreed with Jared's suggestion for a cremation. He'd also proposed delaying the small private service until her parents returned from New Zealand.

While Jared was in L.A., Faith managed to track down her parents at her aunt's house in Auckland. When she'd told them the news about Paula, they'd wanted to fly back immediately, but she'd managed to dissuade them. They'd greeted the news about Nicky with surprise and ultimately joy, and had wanted to know about Jared, who Faith told them was a wonderful father. She also passed along Jared's invitation for them to come for a visit once they returned from New Zealand.

But it was her mother's comments about Paula that stood out most in Faith's memory.

She'd always thought her parents favored Paula, until her mother expressed her sadness over the fact that Paula had always been insecure. She'd told Faith that they'd often despaired that Paula's need for attention would one day be her undoing.

Faith's thoughts were cut off by the sound of the teakettle whistling. Reaching up to open a cabinet, she realized how comfortable and happy she'd become in Jared's home. Her mother had asked her when she was heading back to San Francisco, and Faith hadn't known the answer.

But much as she hated the thought of leaving Nicky, she knew she couldn't stay on indefinitely.

"Are you making tea? I could use a cup," Jared said when he joined her in the kitchen.

"Did you manage to get Nicky to settle down?" she asked, setting the tray with the teapot, two cups and saucers, a cream jug and sugar bowl on the table.

"Yes, finally," Jared replied. "But he's up there in his crib staring at his mobile. He's fascinated with it. I can't believe how much he's grown since we brought him home."

Faith felt her heart falter. Jared was speaking as if they were Nicky's parents, and it was all she could do to control the rush of emotion engulfing her.

She managed a smile. "Next he'll be rolling over, then sitting up, then crawling," she said as she poured tea into the cups.

"Thanks," Jared said, and reached for the cream jug. "And before we know it he'll be asking for the keys to the car and saying he has a date with the prettiest girl in town." He laughed.

The deep rich sound sent a shiver of longing chasing down Faith's spine, and not for the first time she wished she could stay around and watch Nicky grow up to manhood.

She was becoming much too fond of these moments, moments when they talked about Nicky, sharing observations, about how often he smiled, or if he'd shown interest in a new toy.

"Listen, Faith, I know it's only been two weeks since the accident, but we haven't had a chance to sit down and talk." Jared's tone was serious. "I just want to tell you how much I appreciate all you've done for Nicky, and for me."

"Jared, please," Faith interjected. "Having Nicky to look after has helped me a great deal, more than you can ever know."

Jared's gaze held hers for a long moment. "I'm glad," he said. "Losing your sister has been hard enough to deal with. I can't even begin to imagine what you must have gone through when you lost your child."

The sympathy and concern in his voice was almost her undoing. Tears gathered in her eyes.

"Faith, I'm so sorry," Jared said. "I'm a clumsy fool. I didn't mean to upset you." He reached over and covered her hand with his in a gesture that melted her heart.

"I'm fine," she said in a husky voice, wondering how Jared knew about Erica. "Losing someone you love is heartbreaking, but losing a child is like losing a part of yourself," she said. "But I wouldn't change a moment of the five brief but wonderful days I had with my daughter."

"She only lived for five days?" Jared asked, wishing he'd paid closer attention to what his friend DeMarco had told him about Paula's twin sister.

"Yes," Faith replied, gently pulling her hand free.

"At least you had your husband..." he said.

Faith shot him an angry glare. "My husband left when I was four months pregnant. That was the same day the doctors told us the child I was carrying would have little chance of survival. I guess he just couldn't face it," she said, fighting for control.

"You faced it. You were there for your daughter when she needed you. That took courage."

Fresh tears welled up in her eyes and a warmth stole through her at his words. He wasn't at all like Glen; he'd been there for Paula. Jared was a man of much higher caliber.

Not for the first time since Jared had barged into her life, Faith wished things were different, wished Nicky were her son, wished... But wishes rarely come true.

"Did you love your husband very much?" Jared asked, knowing he was prying, but unable to stop himself.

The ghost of a smile curved her mouth. "I was twenty-three when I met him. What did I know about love?" She shook her head. "That's all in the past. What's important is Nicky and what's best for him."

"You've done a wonderful job so far. But we both know things can't go on like this. You have a house and a career waiting for you back in San Francisco. And I can't, in good conscience, allow you to put your life on hold indefinitely. It's time for us both to move on."

Chapter Nine

Faith couldn't breathe. She felt as if someone was squeezing her heart in a vise. Even though she'd known this day was coming, had tried to prepare herself for the inevitability of it, the thought of moving on and leaving Nicky, who was like her own child, was more than she could bear.

She struggled to find her voice. "I suppose you're right," she managed to say, forcing the words past her lips, keeping her gaze focused on the tea cooling in her cup.

"The most practical solution would be to hire a nanny for Nicky."

"A nanny," Faith repeated, lifting the cup to her lips. "How long do you think it will take to find someone suitable?" she asked, ignoring the ache throbbing in her heart.

"I don't know. I thought I'd start by putting an

ad in a few newspapers and go from there. Of course, if you're anxious to get back to San Francisco I can ask Maggie if she could baby-sit Nicky for me during the day."

"No!" The word came out more sharply than she'd intended. "I mean, I'm not in a hurry to get back. I called my publisher yesterday, and he told me he doesn't have anything for me at the moment."

"You don't mind staying on a little longer?"

"No, I don't mind," Faith replied, refraining from adding she'd be happy to stay forever.

Jared smiled, and Faith felt her heart skip a beat in response. "Thank you. You've been more than generous staying as long as you have. And presuming I do get a few replies, would you be willing to look them over? I'd appreciate your input."

"Sure," Faith replied, pleased he'd asked for her help, yet at the same time unhappy she'd be choosing her own replacement.

Jared leaned back in the chair. "So, tell me. How many books have you illustrated?"

"A dozen," Faith said.

"Wow! I'm impressed," Jared said. "What kind of books are they?"

"Children's picture books."

"I'm not too familiar with those," he said. "But having Nicky around will change my reading habits, I imagine." He smiled. "I'd love to see your work. Have you always liked to draw and paint?"

A little disconcerted by his interest, Faith toyed

with her teacup before answering. "From as far back as I can remember I was happiest when I had crayons or pencils and scraps of paper in front of me."

"I, on the other hand, don't have an artistic bone in my body," Jared said. "I can't even draw stick men. Mind you, I was probably one of those kids who had more fun chewing on crayons, rather than drawing with them." He started to laugh.

"I hope your mother took the crayons away before you got sick," Faith said, joining in his laughter. The cheery sound flowed over her, lifting her spirits a notch.

"That was the baby-sitter's job," Jared said off-handedly.

"Baby-sitter," Faith repeated, catching something in his voice. "Did your mother leave you with a baby-sitter often?"

Jared met her gaze, and Faith noticed he was no longer smiling. "As a matter of fact, she left me with a baby-sitter most of my childhood." His tone was ice-cold.

"What about your father? Didn't he ever baby-sit?" she asked lightly, and watched as Jared's mouth tightened into a thin line.

"My father didn't bother to hang around long enough for us to get acquainted."

"Is that why—" Faith broke off abruptly. "Sorry. It's really none of my business."

"Were you going to ask if that was why I was so determined to track Nicky down?"

Faith nodded.

"The answer is yes. I wanted to find my son and bring him home. That's the only way I could be absolutely sure he would receive the kind of love and attention he deserves."

The intensity in his voice startled Faith, but before she could comment he hurried on.

"I didn't want a child of mine to go through what I'd gone through. My mother was a budding actress. She thought nothing of dragging me from audition to audition, or leaving me with strangers at odd hours of the day or night, or dropping me off at a friend's hotel room where I was at times ignored, or worse, neglected." Jared pushed back his chair and stood up.

"How awful!" Faith commented, scarcely able to believe what he'd told her. But there was no mistaking the echo of remembered pain and anger in his voice.

She could see the tension in every line of his body, and for a fleeting second she was tempted to reach out and offer comfort, not to the man, but to the hurt little boy still residing somewhere deep inside.

"I vowed my son would never have to endure a similar fate."

"But Paula wouldn't have dragged Nicky around like that, would she?"

Jared spun around, his eyes ablaze. "Not if I had anything to do with it."

All at once Jared's anger evaporated. He raked a hand through his hair. "I'm sorry. I know the two of you must have been close, but you'd have to agree, when it came to her career, Paula was nothing short of obsessive.'' He sighed. ''There was a time when I'd actually hoped—'' He broke off abruptly. ''This isn't getting us anywhere,'' he said. ''I'd better write up that ad and call it in.''

Faith was silent as she watched Jared leave the kitchen. She'd heard the sorrow and the regret in his voice. What had Jared been hoping for?

Could his anger and frustration simply be a camouflage he used to hide his true feelings for Paula? Had he regarded Paula's return to Grace Harbor as a sign showing her willingness to reach a new understanding, perhaps even a reconciliation?

''Excuse me, Mr. McAndrew. Another fax just came through in response to your ad for a nanny,'' Sally said as she entered Jared's office.

Jared frowned as he looked up from the file he'd been studying. ''What? Sorry, Sally, I wasn't listening.''

''We just received another reply to your ad.''

''Oh...thanks, toss it with the others.'' Jared turned his attention once again to the file.

''Shouldn't you read them?''

Jared glanced up. ''I am reading...oh, you mean the replies,'' he quickly amended. ''I'll get to them later.''

''You said that yesterday and the day before.''

"Did I?" Jared leaned back in his leather chair. "Pass them to me, would you?"

Sally picked up the small bundle of unopened envelopes along with the faxes and gave them to her boss.

"How many replies are there?"

"Five regular letters and three faxes."

Jared scanned the top of his desk in search of the letter opener. "Oh, thanks." He flashed a smile when Sally handed him the brass opener.

"Uh…Mr. McAndrew?" Sally began hesitantly.

"Yes?" Jared slid the opener along the first envelope.

"I'm leaving now for my dental appointment."

"You are?"

Sally sighed. "I told you on Monday I had an appointment with Dr. West Thursday afternoon. That's today," she said, a hint of exasperation in her voice.

"Oh…right! I remember. You'd better be off."

"See you tomorrow," Sally said before withdrawing.

Jared opened the envelopes one by one, and stacked the sheets of paper on top of the faxes. He studied the pile, wondering why he was reluctant to look at them.

With one thing and another, he'd been kept busy for the past two weeks, dealing with a backlog of work. Each night he'd lock up the office and head home, looking forward to spending time with his son, and Faith.

He smiled when he thought of Nicky. He was indeed a happy, contented baby, growing like a weed and changing each and every day.

Silently Jared acknowledged he had Faith to thank for Nicky's happy state. Confident and relaxed with the baby, she was a natural mother, her presence creating a warm and loving atmosphere.

His thoughts lingered on Faith. Since his return from L.A., he'd kept his distance, emotionally and physically, giving her time to grieve, time to heal. He knew she took great solace in the everyday care of the baby.

At times he found himself envying her for the ease with which she handled Nicky during his fussy times. Nothing seemed to fluster her, and while she tried to maintain a schedule of sorts, she wasn't rigid or controlling.

Suddenly the answer to the question of why he wasn't eager to hire a nanny slammed into him with the force of a punch. He didn't want Faith to leave!

Almost from the moment he'd brought her and Nicky home to Grace Harbor, they'd formed a unit, a family, and the thought of her returning to San Francisco brought an ache to his chest.

Faith's generosity in agreeing to stay on to look after Nicky was more than he'd had a right to expect, and he knew she was the reason for the harmony he'd been enjoying. Even in the face of her personal loss she'd held them all together. She was an incredible woman. Not for the first time, Jared was struck by the sharp contrast between Faith and her twin.

Still, there was no getting away from the fact he had Paula to thank for his son. And while her death had shocked and saddened him, Faith had taken the news especially hard.

That's why he'd insisted on flying down to L.A. to take care of everything. He'd felt he owed it to Faith, and to Paula.

He'd paid off her extravagant hotel bill. Money, or rather the lack of it, had been the main reason Paula had contacted him when she'd discovered she was pregnant. She'd told him she'd signed a contract with her agent agreeing not to get pregnant, and she'd been afraid if he found out she was in breach of her contract any hope of a career in Hollywood would go down the drain.

He wasn't altogether sure she was telling the truth, but she'd been desperate to keep her pregnancy under wraps and willing to let him take care of her.

During his two days and nights in L.A., he'd spent a good deal of time taking a long hard look at his relationship with Paula. While he wasn't proud of his irresponsible behavior, neither could he truly regret what had happened between them. How could he? The result had been Nicky.

And he'd missed his son, more than he thought

possible. Missed the nightly ritual of bathing him, feeding him his bottle and rocking him to sleep. But Nicky wasn't the only one Jared missed while in L.A. He'd missed Faith, her quiet reserve, her poise, her warmth, and most of all her smile.

Suddenly Jared's thoughts shifted to the night of the barbecue, recalling how incredibly beautiful Faith had looked and how she'd proved herself to be a wonderful hostess. Her friendly personality and genuine warmth had easily won over his friends.

His intention that night when he'd started flirting with her had simply been to rattle her defenses in the hope she would reveal her true identity and perhaps even tell him what Paula was planning.

By the time their guests departed, he'd convinced himself a kiss was all that was necessary in order to force her into the open.

His plan had backfired the moment his mouth touched hers, because he'd forgotten everything but the woman in his arms.

She'd tasted like heaven, pure and sweet, and her natural sensuality had wound around his heart, pulling him into deep, treacherous waters. The feel of her body pressed hard against his had ignited a need more powerful than anything he'd ever felt before.

When she'd broken the kiss it had taken him all his strength not to haul her back into his arms, but the look of distress and dismay clouding her green eyes had stopped him cold.

His thoughts were cut off when the telephone on

his desk started ringing. With a muffled curse, Jared snatched up the receiver.

"Yes!" he barked.

"Jared? It's me. Is something wrong?" The sound of Faith's anxious voice caught him off guard, and he felt his heart jam against his ribs in response.

"Sorry, Faith. I didn't mean to snap at you."

"I'm sorry to disturb you, Jared, but I was beginning to worry."

In the background Jared could hear Nicky making baby noises. "What time is it?"

"It's almost six-thirty, but—"

"Six-thirty? I guess I lost track of time. Is that Nicky I hear? You haven't given him his bath yet, have you?"

"That's your job. The swimming goggles and snorkel don't fit me, remember?" she teased.

Jared chuckled. "The way Nicky kicks and splashes I've been thinking I should invest in a wet suit."

Faith laughed.

"Thanks for calling. I'll be home soon," Jared said before hanging up.

Faith slowly replaced the receiver. Jared's words echoed in her ears, sending a shiver of longing through her.

Nicky squealed, distracting her, and she turned to smile at him through a haze of tears.

"Your daddy said he'd be home right away," Faith told Nicky, and received a smile in response.

"You love your daddy, don't you?" she cooed. "And he loves you. Yes, he does," she added, and Nicky gurgled with delight.

Faith undid the safety straps and lifted Nicky out of the baby seat. She kissed his cheek, inhaling the scent of baby powder and baby and tried to ignore the little voice inside her head telling her time was running out for her, and there wasn't a thing she could do about it.

"I'd like you to take a look at these," Jared said when he joined Faith in the living room after he'd given Nicky his bath and put him to bed. "They're the replies for the nanny ad," he explained as he dropped the file folder onto the coffee table.

Faith felt her heart skip a beat. "Have you read them?" she asked, leaning forward to retrieve the file.

"That's what I was doing when you called. Have a look and give me your opinion," he said. Crossing to the hearth, he added a log to the fire.

For the next twenty minutes Faith read the letters and accompanying résumés of the eight applicants, finding only four she thought worthy of an interview.

"These four have good references and qualifications," she said, pushing the loose papers across the coffee table toward him. "The others don't have enough experience. At least, that's my opinion."

Jared picked up the letters and studied the four applicants Faith had recommended.

"I agree with you," he said a few moments later. "I'll get Sally to call these women tomorrow and set up interviews." He paused and met her gaze. "Thanks again."

"No problem. Nicky's welfare is important to me," she said, warmed by his words.

"He's going to miss you."

"And I'll miss him." Her voice was husky with repressed emotion. *And I'm going to miss you, Jared,* she added silently, letting her glance slide to the fire, fearful he'd glimpse the look of longing she knew had to be shining in her eyes.

"Of course, you do know you'll be welcome here any time."

"Thank you," Faith managed to respond.

"You amaze me."

Startled, Faith turned to look at him. "I don't understand."

"After all you've been through, you still soldier on."

Tears stung her eyes. "It's been tough, I won't deny it," she said with a watery smile. "But life goes on, and it wouldn't be fair to Nicky to mope around all day and feel sorry for myself."

She stared into the flames and sighed. "Paula and I had our differences, but I loved her. She'll always have a special place in my heart."

"And in mine," Jared said softly.

Pain sliced through her at his comment, which confirmed that he'd hoped Paula's visit might have led to a reconciliation. Tears, ever close to the surface, overflowed and spilled down her cheeks.

Seeing them, Jared threw the letters down on the coffee table and knelt on the floor in front of her, concern and something more etched on his handsome features.

"Faith, I'm sorry. I didn't mean to make you cry."

Brushing the tears aside, Faith shook her head. "I'm fine," she said, all the while wishing he'd take her in his arms and comfort her, just as he'd done the night Paula died.

Faith doubted she would ever forget how it felt to be enfolded in Jared's arms, to feel his warmth, his strength.

"Here." Jared thrust at her a handful of tissues from the box on the end table nearby. Rising, he moved to sit on the seat beside her.

She blew her nose and wiped the moisture from her eyes. Taking a steadying breath, she turned to meet his gaze.

"I'm sorry. I don't know what came over me."

"Hey…don't apologize. Crying is a way of helping to ease the pain and the sorrow."

Silently he berated himself for being the cause of her distress. Lately he seemed to have made a habit of upsetting her.

The urge to take her in his arms and comfort her was almost irresistible, but suddenly he was inexplicably afraid, afraid of the emotions she evoked, afraid simply holding her wouldn't be enough.

Chapter Ten

Faith sat on the sundeck, a sketch pad on her lap. It had rained most of the morning, but the clouds had gradually moved out to sea and the sun was making a valiant effort to brighten up what was left of the day.

She put the finishing touches to the sketch she'd been working on for the past hour, pleased she'd managed to capture the expression of love on Jared's face as he sat in the rocking chair with Nicky in his arms.

Gazing at her detailed drawing, she found herself wishing Jared would look at her that way, then silently she scolded herself for being so fanciful.

Almost a week had passed since she'd read through the applications he'd brought home. She assumed he'd already arranged for interviews, but she couldn't bring herself to ask.

She knew she was avoiding the issue, but the thought of someone else taking care of Nicky, feeding him his bottle, rocking him to sleep, loving him, tore at her heart.

When the peal of the doorbell echoed through the house, Faith closed her sketch pad and hurried inside. Dropping the pad on the kitchen table, she headed for the front door.

"Maggie! Hi. How are you?" Faith asked.

"I'm fine!" Maggie responded. "I hope this isn't a bad time."

"Ah…no. It's lovely to see you. Please, come in."

"I hope you don't mind me dropping by without calling first," Maggie said as she stepped inside.

"Of course not," Faith replied, glad of the company, but unsure just what to say. Jared had told her he'd planned to talk to Dylan and Maggie and explain to them she would be leaving. But Faith wasn't sure if Jared had gotten around to it yet, or of just how much he'd shared.

"You didn't bring Dylan junior with you," Faith said, disappointed not to see the little boy. "Has the tooth he's been cutting finally come through?"

"Would you believe I was up several times during the night with him, and this morning we noticed both bottom teeth had made an appearance."

"I guess that explains why he's been so out of sorts lately. Poor little guy."

"What about poor little me?" Maggie joked as she followed Faith to the kitchen. "I told Dylan I'd be back in ten minutes. I just needed some female company for a change."

Faith flashed a knowing grin over her shoulder. "Do you have enough time for a cup of tea?"

"Sure," Maggie replied with a smile. Sliding off her raincoat, she dropped it over one of the kitchen chairs. "Where's Nicky?" she asked as she sat down.

"He's napping," Faith replied, moving to the sink.

"Jared says you're leaving," Maggie said.

"That's right." Faith darted her a cautious glance.

"Jared also told us, though he really didn't have to, why you're leaving," Maggie went on.

"Oh, I see." It was all Faith could think to say. If Maggie and Dylan knew she wasn't Paula, that she'd been impersonating her twin, she couldn't blame Maggie if she was upset or angry at having been deceived.

"You know, it's funny, but from the moment you answered the phone that day, I knew there was something different about you."

"Maggie, I'm sorry. I hope you can forgive me for deceiving you. My only excuse is, I thought I was doing what was best for Nicky."

"I understand. Truly I do. Jared admitted he should never have let us believe he and Paula were married. He knew it was wrong, but I suppose in his own way he was just trying to protect his unborn child."

Faith nodded, pleased for Jared's sake his friends were so generous and understanding.

"Faith…may I call you Faith?"

"Of course."

"I just want to say how sorry we are about Paula's death. And sorry, too, that you'll be leaving."

"Thank you," Faith managed to say. She didn't deserve Maggie's understanding, but she was glad of it all the same.

"What's this?" Maggie suddenly asked.

Faith turned in time to see Maggie flip open the sketch pad she'd tossed on the table.

"These are really good. Jared mentioned you were an illustrator for children's books. Is that right?"

"Yes," Faith said, wishing she could snatch the pad away before Maggie reached the sketch of Jared.

"Wow! This one of Jared and Nicky is wonderful." Maggie's tone was sincere. "You've drawn them with such love…." She stopped abruptly and looked up at Faith. "Has Jared seen this?"

"No!" Faith replied a little too loudly. She crossed to the table. "Besides, they're just scribbles," she added as she placed a cup and saucer in front of Maggie.

Reaching for the sketch pad, Faith closed it and pushed it aside, aware all the while that Maggie was watching her.

"Jared said he's hiring a nanny for Nicky."

Faith drew a steadying breath. "Yes." She returned to the stove and after dropping a tea bag into the teapot, filled it from the kettle. "In fact, he'll be interviewing prospective candidates very soon—if he hasn't already. And once he's chosen someone, I'll be heading back to San Francisco," Faith added, keeping her tone light.

"Is that really what you want? To go back to San Francisco, I mean?"

"Yes," Faith responded easily, though she avoided meeting Maggie's eyes as she set the teapot on the table. "Why do you ask?"

"Because after seeing that sketch you drew of Jared, I'd say leaving here is the last thing you want to do."

Faith darted a startled glance at her friend. "I don't understand."

"It's really quite obvious."

"What's obvious?" Faith asked, frowning now.

Maggie smiled. "That you're in love with Jared, of course!"

Faith inhaled sharply. "That's ridiculous!"

"Is it?" Maggie countered, smiling at her.

"I'm not in love with Jared," Faith stated with a calmness she was far from feeling. "I mean, I can't be in love with Jared," she added, sounding far less confident. "I don't want to be in love with Jared," she insisted, but her voice lacked conviction.

With each denial Maggie's smile had grown wider, and suddenly Faith realized Maggie was right. She loved Jared, loved everything about him—his smile, his warmth, his strength, his compassion and most of all his commitment to Nicky.

"I think it's wonderful," Maggie said as she poured tea into the two cups. "And as for Jared, I've never seen him happier."

Faith felt like crying. "Maggie? What am I going to do?" Despair edged her voice.

Before Maggie could answer, the telephone rang.

"That's probably Dylan. I'd better take a rain check on the tea." Maggie jumped to her feet and reached for her raincoat. "Tell him I'm on my way," she added as the phone rang a second time. "Oh, and Faith." Maggie slowed to a halt. "Jared's a very lucky man."

Faith managed a weak smile as she reached for the receiver. "Hello!"

"Faith? Rupert Berrisford here. I hope I haven't caught you at a bad time."

"Mr. Berrisford! This is a surprise," Faith responded. She'd called her editor, Brad Potter, a few days ago to let him know where he could reach her, but she certainly hadn't expected to hear from Rupert Berrisford, the managing editor of Berrisford Publishers.

"A pleasant one, I hope," Rupert Berrisford said. "I wanted to be the one to call and give you the news."

"News?"

"We've had a request from one of our renowned authors asking if you'd be interested in doing the illustrations for his newest project," he told her.

"Really?" Faith said, trying to sound suitably impressed. "Who is the author?"

"Jake Jones."

"Jake Jones? The man who writes those delightful and funny children's picture books?" Faith asked, trying not to sound too excited. This was the opportunity of a lifetime.

"Jake has come up with a brand-new character. He's very excited about it, and we, as his publishers, are excited, too. He told me how much he admires your work, and he'd like you to read his latest manuscript and submit drawings for the project. Are you interested?"

Faith couldn't seem to find her voice. Her head was spinning, still trying to digest the news that Jake Jones admired her work.

"Of course, I'm interested," she exclaimed, excitement vibrating through her voice.

"Good. That wasn't too difficult, was it?" Berrisford said, his tone amused. "And Faith, just let me say both Brad and I have every confidence in you and your work. We know you're up to the challenge."

"Thank you, Mr. Berrisford," Faith said, warmed by the support.

"We'll set things in motion. It might take a week or two. Jake is in Colorado at the moment, but as soon as he gets back I'll get Brad to contact you to tell you when to expect the manuscript."

"Fine. And thanks again, Mr. Berrisford."

Faith slowly replaced the receiver. She should be

bouncing off the walls. But already she could feel her excitement, like a balloon with a slow leak, beginning to dissipate. She'd just been offered the opportunity of a lifetime, the chance to work with a writer she greatly admired, so why did she feel so lost and empty inside?

Because it wasn't enough, a voice inside her head replied. Maggie had forced her to face the truth, a truth she'd been avoiding.

She loved Jared, loved him with a depth of emotion she'd never felt before, and while her work brought her a great deal of satisfaction, what she really wanted was to stay in Grace Harbor and be a mother to Nicky, and a wife to the man who was his father.

It was almost five-thirty when Jared walked through from the garage. The smell of garlic and oregano drifted toward him, the appetizing aroma making his mouth water.

As he strode toward the kitchen he heard the sound of someone singing. The sight of Faith, dressed in hip-hugging jeans and a pale blue sweater, waltzing around the work island carrying Nicky in her arms brought him to a halt.

She'd never looked more beautiful, or more desirable. Her eyes sparkled like diamonds, her cheeks were a delicate pink, her mouth…ah…her mouth.

He'd had a brief taste of heaven the night he'd kissed her, a kiss he'd been unable to erase from his memory, a kiss so sensual, so erotic, so wild, just the thought of it made his body grow taut with need.

Of late, he hadn't been sleeping well, plagued by dreams of Faith, of kissing her, of making passionate love to her. Dreams so vivid he'd awakened each morning in a tangle of sheets, his arms empty, his heart aching.

"Is this a private party or can anyone join in?" Jared asked, keeping his tone light and trying to ignore the desire clawing at his insides.

At the sound of Jared's deep, resonant voice, Faith stopped dancing and her heart slammed against her rib cage in startled reaction. It was all she could do to keep her smile pinned firmly in place.

She turned to greet him. "Hi. We didn't hear you come in," she said, hoping he wouldn't notice the color seeping into her cheeks. "I was showing Nicky how to waltz," she explained a little breathlessly.

Jared smiled. "Don't you think he's a bit young for dancing lessons? Shouldn't he learn to walk first?"

The glint of amusement in Jared's eyes sent Faith's blood sprinting through her veins, reawakening needs she'd all but forgotten.

Fearful Jared would see the longing in her eyes, she turned back to Nicky. "You enjoyed your dancing lesson, didn't you, darling?" she asked the baby, who smiled and gurgled in response.

Jared laughed. "Do you know, I've always

wanted to learn to waltz. Maybe you'd like to teach me a step or two.''

Faith felt her mouth go dry at his suggestion. The thought of being held in Jared's arms, their bodies touching, did strange things to her insides.

''Sorry, dance class is over for today,'' she said, a faint huskiness in her voice. ''Here…could you put Nicky in his cuddle seat while I get dinner on the table?''

A few minutes later Faith served up two steaming plates of spaghetti, together with a green salad and garlic bread.

''This sauce is delicious. I'm curious. Where did you learn to cook?''

''My mother taught us when we were growing up.''

''Your mother taught you and Paula to cook?''

''Well, that was the idea. But while Paula did make an effort, she wasn't interested in anything unless it had to do with acting or performing.''

''Having twins must have been hard on your mother. I know how much work one baby is,'' he added, flashing a smile at Nicky, who was waving a rattle.

''My father helped a lot. But my mother did complain now and then about us being a bit of a handful, especially Paula. She was much more adventurous, sometimes reckless.…'' Faith ground to a halt.

''Faith, I'm sorry.'' Jared said.

''No, it's all right,'' she assured him, summoning a smile. ''It makes me feel sad that even though she was my sister, my twin, we weren't as close as I'd have liked.

"She was always eager to try new things, and got rather impatient with me when I wouldn't go along with her.

"I could never quite understand why she wanted to be an actress," Faith continued. "After we graduated from high school we drifted apart. I guess I should have been more supportive, kept in closer touch with her, tried harder...." Her voice cracked.

"You're being too hard on yourself," Jared said softly. "You weren't responsible for what Paula chose to do with her life. She knew what she wanted and she went after it, and while her priorities might have been different than yours or mine, give her credit for having the courage and determination to follow her dream."

Jared was being both kind and forgiving, and again she was left with the impression he'd been willing to take Paula back, to work out their differences, in order to keep their family intact.

Suddenly Nicky let out a frustrated cry and Jared, who'd finished eating, turned to his son.

"I think this little guy is trying to tell me it's time for his bath," Jared said as he bent to lift Nicky from the cuddle seat. "You want your bath, don't you? Now, where did I put my snorkel?"

Nicky's squeal in response to his father's voice made Faith smile, but as she rose from her chair to gather up the dishes, she couldn't ignore the ache throbbing in her heart.

* * *

"Nicky was one tired baby, tonight," Jared commented when he joined Faith in the kitchen half an hour later. "Thanks for bringing his bottle upstairs," he added as he moved to stand beside her at the sink.

"You're welcome," Faith responded as a ripple of awareness danced across her skin in reaction to his nearness.

"Thanks for dinner. It was delicious, by the way, and thanks, too, for cleaning up." He rinsed Nicky's bottle under the tap.

Intent on putting some distance between them, Faith grabbed the tea towel and took a step back. "A dishwasher makes things a lot easier," she said, retreating a little farther.

Jared deftly snagged the loose end of the tea towel and began to dry his hands.

Faith let go her end as if it were on fire. Although he hadn't actually touched her, Jared was much too close for comfort. Her heart started to race, and suddenly she felt an overwhelming longing to feel his body pressed solidly against hers.

"I fancy a glass of wine. Would you care to join me?" he asked. "There's a bottle in the wine rack behind you." He took a step closer.

Her intention was to duck under his arm and make her escape, but she misjudged how close Jared was and instead of avoiding him their bodies collided.

"Whoa!" Jared said at the contact.

The impact sent Faith staggering backward, and

she would have bumped against the counter but for Jared's lightning reflexes. He grabbed her and hauled her back into the safety of his arms.

Crushed against his lean, muscular frame, Faith could neither move nor breathe. For several seconds they stood locked in a passionless embrace.

Only moments ago, she'd been longing to feel his body against hers. Her wish had been granted and it felt a little like heaven. Faith closed her eyes.

"Faith? Are you all right?" Jared asked, concern and something more in his voice.

She drew a deep breath. "I think so." The collision had jarred her, but Jared's nearness and the emotions he'd aroused were infinitely more disturbing.

The heady male scent of him swirled around her, playing havoc with her senses, stirring forgotten longings.

"Perhaps you'd better sit down," he suggested, but when he began to ease her out of his arms, she swayed drunkenly.

All at once the room tipped crazily as her feet left the floor. To her astonishment she realized Jared, like a gallant knight of old, had lifted her into his arms.

Without a word, he carried her through to the living room, and with a tenderness that brought tears to her eyes, he lowered her onto the leather chesterfield.

"Is that better?" he asked, concern and something more in his voice.

"Yes, thank you," Faith replied. "You just knocked the wind out of me, that's all."

Jared settled on the edge of the seat. "Are you sure that's all it was?" His gaze was intense, sending a ripple of need pulsing through her.

Faith couldn't breathe, much less find her voice. Locked in his heated gaze, she watched in fascination as an emotion she couldn't decipher flickered in the depths of his blue eyes. Her mouth went dry and her heart shuddered to a halt as Jared slowly closed the gap between them.

Jared was drawn like the proverbial moth to a flame. The need to find out if the memory of their kiss was equal to the real thing was suddenly more than he could resist.

His memory had failed him badly. The difference between this and the dreams that had begun to haunt him recently was like night and day.

The explosion of heat and desire engulfing him rocked him to the core. She tasted of sweetness and innocence, mystery and mayhem, sensuality and sensitivity, and when her mouth opened under his in eager invitation, the temptation to lose himself completely almost overwhelmed him.

Faith responded to Jared's kiss with all the love she had in her heart. She wanted him, needed him desperately, and as he deepened the kiss, compelling them closer to the edge of reason, she reveled in the knowledge he wanted her, too.

When his mouth left hers to forge a hot, wet path to her ear, she whimpered in protest.

"Do you have any idea what you're doing to me?" Jared's voice was husky with desire.

"Yes! Because you're doing the same to me. Jared, please...I need you." Faith's plea was barely audible as desire bubbled through her like molten lava.

Jared felt his control slipping away. He'd never known such an all-consuming desire, never felt the depth of emotion this woman managed to evoke.

Until now, he'd always kept a tight rein on his heart, priding himself in being able to keep his deepest emotions in check, never allowing anyone to get too close.

From a very early age he'd learned that emotional involvements only made a person vulnerable and ultimately brought nothing but pain and heartache.

The feelings he had for Faith were far stronger than anything he'd felt before. She was leading him into uncharted waters, into territory that was new and decidedly dangerous.

For the first time in his life, he was afraid. Afraid of how much he cared, afraid of what he might have found with Faith, afraid of what he might ultimately lose.

Jared drew a ragged breath. He wanted her, yes, but he was afraid to take the chance of revealing just how much he needed her...loved her.

He pulled free of Faith's arms and stood up, silently telling himself he was doing the right thing, that he would only end up hurting her.

A chill ran through him at the look of surprise and bewilderment that appeared in her eyes.

"I'm sorry, Faith, I can't do this," he said, a slight tremor in his voice. "It's not you, it's me—" He broke off and raked his hands through his hair. His thoughts were jumbled, his body aching with need, but he struggled to find the right words. "You're so different. You're not Paula, and I—"

Faith's startled gasp brought him to a halt. The look of pain darkening her eyes tore at his heart and he knew he'd bungled it.

"Faith! No…that's not what I meant.… You don't understand—"

"You're wrong, Jared," Faith said as she quickly scrambled to her feet. Her heart was breaking, her body still throbbing with the need he'd aroused. "I understand perfectly," she said, and without another word she turned and ran from the room.

Chapter Eleven

Faith stumbled up the stairs. She didn't stop until she'd reached the sanctuary of her room. Closing the door, she leaned against it and slowly slid to the floor. Only then did she let the tears fall.

Lowering her head to her knees, she wept. There was little joy in knowing she'd been right. Jared had loved Paula, was still in love with Paula.

He'd kissed her only because she reminded him of her twin, and she was a fool to think he'd been attracted to her for any other reason.

Faith took several deep breaths. It didn't help that being in Jared's arms had felt so wonderful, so right. The passion his kiss had ignited still hummed through her system. She'd never experienced such an overpowering desire before, and she very much doubted she would again.

The thought of facing Jared after what had happened between them brought a moan to her lips. Only a few hours ago she'd wanted to stay in Grace Harbor forever. Now she couldn't wait to leave. She told herself returning to San Francisco was best for everyone, and suddenly her upcoming project with Jake Jones looked like her salvation.

A knock on her bedroom door startled her.

"Faith! Please open the door. We need to talk." The sound of Jared's voice sent a quiver of remembered need through her. Hugging her knees to her chest, she held her breath.

"Faith! Please."

She made no reply, sure he must hear the drumming of her heart. When at last she heard the soft tread of his footsteps moving down the hall, she sighed with relief.

Faith spent a miserable night, dozing fitfully. It was still dark when she glanced at the clock on her bedside table. It was almost seven. For the past hour she'd been staring at the ceiling.

She knew it was cowardly to run, and the thought of leaving Nicky tore at her heart, but after the disastrous encounter with Jared last night, she needed to get away and lick her wounds in private.

Besides, Jared was quite capable of looking after Nicky, and with the weekend approaching, he'd manage on his own for a few days.

Although he hadn't said as much, she assumed he'd already interviewed all four candidates for the job of nanny. She was confident he'd have no trouble choosing one. She could only hope the new nanny would be available to start soon.

When Nicky started to cry, Faith automatically pushed back the covers and climbed out of bed, but as she reached the door she heard Jared's heavy tread in the hallway.

Any other morning she would have gone downstairs and warmed Nicky's bottle and brought it up to the nursery for him. She'd enjoyed those precious times they spent together, like a real family. But her fantasy was just that, a fantasy, and she'd been a fool to think it could be anything else.

Faith headed for the shower. She wasn't looking forward to facing Jared. Standing under the hot spray, she wished she could wave her hand and somehow magically whisk herself back to San Francisco.

After pulling on her jeans and sweater, she plugged in the hair dryer. A few minutes later she heard a loud knock on her bedroom door.

Ignoring Jared would be rude and juvenile, she told herself, and so she switched off the hair dryer, and crossed to the door.

Jared stood in the hall dressed in a double-breasted slate gray suit, white shirt and striped tie. His hair glistened with moisture, his jaw looked smooth and inviting, and the scent of lime and leather tickled her nostrils, sending her pulse into overdrive.

"Sorry to bother you." Jared said. "I've already changed Nicky and given him his bottle. I'm driving to Newport this morning to meet with a client. But I couldn't leave without making sure you were all right and to say I'm sorry about last night."

"Don't be…" Faith quickly responded, the pain of his rejection returning full force. "We've both been under stress lately," she said, wishing he would go.

"That's true, but we still need to talk," he insisted. "I'd like to explain—"

"There's nothing to explain."

"I disagree," Jared countered, frustration edging his voice. "I wish I could stay and sort this out now, but I have to go. Can we talk later?"

Faith could only nod in response. The ball of emotion lodged in her throat made it impossible for her to speak. Besides, he didn't have to explain. She already knew the reason he'd rejected her. He couldn't love her because he was still in love with her twin sister, the mother of his child.

After Jared left, Faith finished blow-drying her hair before checking on Nicky. He lay in his crib kicking his legs and waving his arms, intrigued as always by the mobile circling above his head.

Faith spent the next hour tending to him. She sang to him as she bathed him, she made him smile, delighting in the child who had given her back her peace of mind and melted the ice around her heart.

When Nicky dozed off, Faith headed downstairs, noticing through the kitchen window that it had started snowing.

She located the phone book and dialed the number for Grace Harbor's bus depot. She voiced her question, and was politely told buses for Portland left at eleven, one and three every day, while buses to Seattle left at noon, two and four.

Faith hung up and glanced at the clock. It was almost ten. Portland was out, she decided, but she could easily catch the bus to Seattle at noon.

With two hours to get organized, she picked up the phone, dialed Maggie's number and asked her friend if she could look after Nicky for a few hours.

After packing the items she'd brought with her, Faith saw that Nicky had awakened from his nap. She dressed him and played with him, prolonging these last precious moments, not knowing when she would see him again.

Outside it was still snowing. Faith was surprised to see there was already an accumulation of about an inch on the ground, but she decided to walk the short distance with Nicky to Maggie and Dylan's house anyway.

Even though Maggie invited her to stay, Faith politely declined, knowing she had to get going. "Just let me give Nicky a goodbye kiss," Faith said, reaching for the baby.

As she lifted Nicky into her arms she felt tears prick her eyes. Burying her face in the folds of his jacket, she hugged and kissed the baby she'd come to love like her own son. "Goodbye, my darling," she whispered against his cheek.

"Faith? Are you all right?" Maggie asked.

"I'm fine," Faith replied, blinking back tears.

"You'd think you were leaving him here forever," Maggie teased, taking Nicky once more.

Faith summoned a smile. "I'd better go."

"See you a little later. Mind how you go."

"I will," Faith replied, managing to smile again. Slipping outside, she closed the door behind her.

Faith stood on the doorstep for several seconds, struggling to suppress the sob rising in her throat, telling herself over and over she would have all the time in the world to cry once she was back in San Francisco.

When she reached the end of the driveway, she picked up her knapsack from where she'd left it and hurried down Indigo Street, oblivious to the snow falling like confetti around her. By the time she reached the bus station she was wet and cold. After buying her ticket to Seattle, she glanced at the clock. The bus was scheduled to leave in ten minutes.

Crossing to the small bank of phones, she dropped in a quarter and dialed Jared's number. She waited for the answering machine to pick up, and at the sound of Jared's voice a fresh wave of pain washed over her. Gripping the receiver tightly in her hand, she took a deep breath.

"Jared, it's Faith. Nicky's with Maggie. By the time you get this message I'll be on my way to San Francisco. We both know it's for the best. Goodbye."

She hung up and walked outside to board the bus.

"Any messages?" Jared asked as he swept into the office, brushing snow from his coat.

"They're on your desk," Sally said.

Jared slid off his coat and tossed it on the chair in his office. Picking up the pile of message slips, he thumbed through them.

He'd just arrived back from Newport. The meeting hadn't gone at all well, due to the fact he'd been distracted by thoughts of Faith and the kiss they'd shared the night before.

He wished he hadn't had an appointment, wished he'd had a chance to talk to her. He'd seen the redness in her eyes, a sure sign she'd spent the night crying.

Jared smiled ruefully. He still couldn't get Faith out of his mind, nor her wild response to his kiss, a response that had sent his world spinning out of control.

Dropping into his chair, Jared reached for the phone. After punching in his own number, he listened to the phone ringing in his house. As he waited, he drummed his fingers impatiently on his desk.

When the answering machine kicked in he replaced the receiver and leaned back, his expression thoughtful. Why hadn't Faith answered?

She was probably feeding Nicky, he told himself calmly. Or maybe she'd taken him for a walk. No, that was unlikely—it was snowing outside.

Jared sighed and turned his attention once again to his phone messages. He flipped through them a second time, then with a muttered curse threw them on his desk.

He leaned his elbows on his desk, lowered his head onto his hands and closed his eyes. An image of Faith swam before him, a look of bewilderment and pain on her face. It was the same expression he'd seen when he'd abruptly put a stop to their lovemaking last night.

Jared drew a ragged breath. Why had he stopped making love to the most beautiful, most exciting and most incredible woman he'd ever known?

He'd never felt this way before, about anyone. Light romantic entanglements lasting a few weeks or sometimes a few months were more his line, for the simple reason that they left his heart intact.

But somehow Faith had managed to slip beneath his defenses and capture his heart. He'd fallen in love with her! And it scared him to death.

Love was an emotion he'd made a point of avoiding. He'd learned at an early age loving someone only led to pain and heartache.

But the moment Faith had come on the scene the rules had changed. And while the love he felt for his son ran very deep, the love he felt for Faith was more powerful by far.

"I'm in love with her," Jared said with quiet conviction. "I'm in love with her," he repeated.

Reaching for the phone, he punched the redial button. His heart began to pound and a feeling of joy washed over him as he waited for Faith to pick up. When he heard his recorded message, he cursed soundly and slammed down the receiver.

A few minutes later he snatched up the phone

again and called Maggie, who told him that Faith had left Nicky with her for a few hours.

"Did she tell you where she was going?" Jared asked.

"No, she didn't say," Maggie replied. "She seemed upset when she left. She hugged and kissed Nicky like she wasn't coming back."

Jared froze. "Thanks, Maggie. I'll be by to pick up Nicky later."

He replaced the receiver, his thoughts in chaos. Faith was leaving town! It was the only explanation. And after last night's debacle, he couldn't really blame her.

Jared jumped up, and grabbing his coat, ran out of his office and hurriedly raced over the snow-covered sidewalk to where he'd parked his car. The bus depot! She had to have headed there, he surmised. Buses were the only means of transportation out of town.

Jared pulled out of the parking spot, but he hadn't driven one block when he was forced to slow to a crawl. The snow was snarling traffic, and the main street was already backed up. He sat at the first traffic light for almost five minutes before the line of cars finally began to move forward.

When he pulled up outside the bus depot, the digital clock on the dashboard read 1:58.

Leaving the car engine running, he tramped through the snow toward the ticket office.

"When's the next bus to Portland?" he asked the clerk.

"It left an hour ago," she replied.

"An hour ago—" Jared's heart sank. Through the windows of the shelter he could see three buses parked outside. "Are those buses scheduled to leave any time soon?"

"Only number twelve. It's going to Seattle. The driver should be pulling out any minute now."

Jared spun around and raced outside. He slid his way toward the first bus. The door was closed. Jared slapped his hand on the door, praying the driver wouldn't ignore him.

The door opened and the driver greeted Jared with a friendly smile. "You're a lucky man—you're right on time."

"I hope so," Jared said as he climbed aboard. "Don't go anywhere for a minute. I'm looking for someone." He moved down the aisle, scanning the faces of the dozen or so passengers on board, searching for Faith.

Over the top of the seats he glimpsed a familiar figure sitting near the rear of the bus. Relief swamped him when he saw Faith staring dejectedly out of the window.

She turned and as their gazes collided, Jared caught the flicker of joy that danced for a brief moment in her eyes.

"Jared, what are you doing here?" she asked.

"Faith, please don't go."

Tears pooled in her beautiful eyes. "It's no use. I can't stay." She averted her gaze.

"We need to talk. Please, Faith I don't want you to go."

Faith shook her head.

"Hey, buddy," the driver said. "What gives? Are you staying on or getting off?"

Jared glanced over his shoulder at the driver. "We're getting off." He turned to Faith. "If you still want to leave after you hear what I have to say, I promise you I'll drive you anywhere you want to go."

"Lady, that's a pretty nice offer," the bus driver commented. "Give the guy a break! Hell, give me a break! I'm liable to lose my job unless I get this bus on the road in the next two minutes."

Faith hesitated. "All right," she agreed, relenting, and started to get up.

"Give me your knapsack," Jared said. He stepped back, then followed her off the bus.

"My car's over here," Jared said and, cupping her elbow, urged her forward, praying silently someone hadn't driven off with his car. Behind them the bus pulled out.

His car was still there. He opened his door and flicked the switch to unlock the others. Tossing her knapsack in the back seat, he climbed in and waited for Faith to join him.

"Where are we going?" Faith asked a few minutes later once she was in the passenger seat.

"Home," Jared replied, turning the car in the direction he'd come.

It had stopped snowing by the time they reached

the house. Faith was already beginning to have second thoughts, scolding herself for not putting up more resistance. What could Jared possibly have to say that would change her mind?

Jared activated the garage door opener, then drove inside. A shiver chased down Faith's spine. It seemed like only yesterday she'd arrived here for the first time. In truth it was closer to six weeks.

Once inside, Jared shrugged off his coat and helped Faith off with hers. "Let's go through to the living room." He tossed both coats over the newel post.

Faith led the way. She crossed the carpeted floor and came to a halt in front of the fireplace.

She turned. "Jared, I don't think—"

"You agreed to hear me out."

"All right." She glanced at the chesterfield, where only last night Jared had kissed her. She chose the easy chair instead.

She watched Jared draw a deep breath then slowly release it. He sat down opposite her, and clasping his hands together, he leaned toward her, capturing her gaze.

"Last night..." The words came out in a hoarse whisper. He coughed and started again. "Last night when I brought a halt to...uh...what was happening between us, you thought it was because you reminded me of Paula. It's not true. You and Paula couldn't be more different. That was the whole problem."

Faith frowned, unable to understand what he meant. But before she could speak, he hurried on.

"You are the most unselfish, generous, warm-hearted, caring, loyal, devoted, beautiful, sexy woman I have ever met. And if I hadn't been so damned angry the day I found you and Nicky in San Francisco, if I hadn't been so caught up in finding my son, I'd have realized right away you weren't Paula.

"Yes, Paula and I were lovers, but we were never in love. I didn't believe in love. Didn't want to believe in love." He paused for breath. "Until I met you."

Faith felt her heart leap into her throat. "Wha...what are you saying?"

"Bringing you to Grace Harbor was the best thing I ever did. Ever since you came into my life you've taught me what it is to be part of a family. These past weeks have been the happiest I've ever known.

"I've never felt this way about anyone," he went on. "And I don't mind admitting it scares the hell out of me. That's why I stopped last night...because what I feel for you scares me." He stood up and began to pace.

He stopped and spun around to face her. "I think I'm in love with you. Hopelessly, madly in love with you. And the thought of you not being in my life, in our lives, is more than I can stand."

Faith couldn't find her voice. Had Jared said what she thought he'd said? She looked up at him and saw the fear and the love etched on his handsome face.

"You've heard me out. If you want to leave, I'll take you wherever you want to go."

"What makes you think I want to leave?" Faith asked, suddenly locating her courage and her voice.

Jared dragged a hand through his hair. "Because I've made a proper botch of things, I suppose." He sighed. "For all I know you were heading back to pick up with your ex-husband...." His voice trailed off.

Faith leapt to her feet. "You must be joking!" she said, aghast he'd even think such a thing.

"I'm sorry," he quickly apologized, and Faith saw hope flicker, like a candle, in his eyes.

"I'm not still in love with Glen," she told him. "I thought I made that clear. I doubt I was ever in love with him. I think I fell in love with love because I wanted so badly to be loved."

Jared took a step toward her, then stopped.

"Do you think you could ever fall in love with me?" he asked, and Faith's heart burst with love at the vulnerability reflected in his voice and in his eyes.

"Oh, Jared...don't you know I already have?"

Suddenly she was in his arms, his mouth devouring hers. Faith willingly gave herself up to the heat and passion erupting, like a long-dormant volcano, between them.

It was several minutes before Jared let her up for

air. He drew away, but kept her in the tight circle of his arms.

"I love you, Faith. More than I thought I could love anyone."

"And I love you," she replied, scarcely able to believe this was really happening.

"After we get married, would moving in here be a problem for you, as far as your career goes, I mean? Because we could easily relocate to San Francisco."

"As far as my work is concerned, it doesn't matter where I live. What's important is that we're together," she added, warmed by his concern. "By the way, was that an official proposal?" she teased.

Jared laughed, the low rumble of sound doing strange things to her pulse.

"No, but this is." With a flourish he knelt at her feet and kissed her hand. "My darling Faith, will you do me the honor of becoming my wife?"

Faith blinked away the tears blurring her eyes. "Yes! Oh, Jared! Yes!" she answered, her voice husky with emotion. She urged him to his feet and met his hungry mouth with her own.

Beneath her splayed fingers she could feel his heart beating in a rhythm that matched hers. With some effort she drew away, delighting in the love and desire she could see shining in his eyes.

"We should go and get Nicky."

"You're right." Jared kissed her forehead. "We have something very special here, Faith, and Nicky's a big part of it. Yes, Paula had her faults, but I keep thinking you wouldn't be here in my arms right now if I'd never met her.'' He smiled and kissed her nose.

"When Nicky's old enough to understand," he continued, "we'll tell him the story of how his mother brought us together."

Faith's throat tightened with emotion, making it impossible for her to speak.

"I'm truly sorry Paula never got the chance to realize her dreams. She would have made one hell of an actress. I just wish I knew why she was coming back. Was it for Nicky?"

Faith drew a steadying breath. "I asked her to come," she told him, and watched his pupils widen with surprise. "I thought she ought to tell you in person what she'd decided to do about Nicky. She owed it to you, and to me.

"She put me in a very awkward position. And let me tell you I wasn't exactly thrilled at the thought of having to play the role of counterfeit wife."

Jared had the good grace to look remorseful. "I should never have misled my friends about my relationship with Paula. I wasn't thinking straight." He brought her hand to his mouth and kissed her palm, an action that robbed her of breath and sent a quiver of need racing through her.

"Did you say counterfeit wife?" he asked, drawing her closer.

Faith nodded.

"I'm sorry, but a counterfeit wife won't do at all. I want the real thing," he said.

"I'm so glad," Faith said, and as Jared's mouth captured hers once more, she responded with all the love in her heart, knowing she'd found true happiness at last.

Epilogue

Two Years Later

Faith followed Jared as he carried Nicky upstairs to bed. Nicky was asleep in his father's arms.

Jared lowered Nicky onto his new bed and tucked in the covers. Smiling at the sleeping figure, he dropped a kiss on his son's forehead. "Night, sport."

Faith traded places with her husband and, brushing several strands of hair off Nicky's forehead, she kissed a rosy cheek. "Night, poppet. Sleep tight. We love you."

Faith followed Jared down the hall to their bedroom.

"Darling? What time are Maggie and Dylan picking us up?" Faith asked as she crossed to the dresser.

"In about an hour. Why?"

Faith turned and smiled. "And Jenny doesn't get here for another forty minutes, right?"

Jared frowned. "I suppose," he said cautiously.

"Good. That gives me plenty of time," Faith said, her smile widening.

"Time for what?" Jared asked, and caught a glint of amusement and something else in his wife's green eyes.

"For me to give you your present." Faith watched her husband close the gap between them, a quizzical expression on his handsome face.

"What present? It's not my birthday." Jared drew her into his arms and starting kissing the sensitive spot just below her right ear.

Faith's breath hitched. Sliding her arms around his neck, she swayed against him, her body already growing feverish with anticipation.

"What present?" He whispered the question into her ear, his hot breath sending a shiver through her.

"We're going to have a baby."

At her words Jared froze, then he pulled back to look into her eyes. His mouth opened and closed several times, but no sound emerged.

Faith smiled and nodded. "We're going to have a baby. Nicky's going to have a new brother or a sister. You're going to be a daddy again. We're going to be parents...."

Jared silenced her with a kiss, a kiss so tender, so loving and so full of reverence, he stole her heart all over again.

"How long have you known?"

"Since this morning," she replied, enjoying herself.

"Do we really have to go out tonight?" he complained before his tongue made a foray into her ear. "Couldn't we stay home and...uh...celebrate?"

Faith laughed softly. "I suppose. Why don't you call Maggie."

Jared sighed. "How much time did you say we had?"

"A lifetime," Faith replied before finding his mouth with hers.

* * * * *

SOMETIMES THE SMALLEST PACKAGES CAN LEAD TO THE BIGGEST SURPRISES!

February 1999
A VOW, A RING, A BABY SWING
by Teresa Southwick (SR #1349)

Pregnant and alone, Rosie Marchetti had just been stood up at the altar.
So family friend Steve Schafer stepped up the aisle and married her.
Now Rosie is trying to convince him that this family was meant to be....

May 1999
THE BABY ARRANGEMENT
by Moyra Tarling (SR #1368)

Jared McAndrew has been searching for his son, and when he discovers
Faith Nelson with his child he demands she come home with him. Can
Faith convince Jared that he has the wrong mother—but the right bride?

Enjoy these stories of love and family. And look for future
BUNDLES OF JOY titles from Leanna Wilson and Suzanne McMinn
coming in the fall of 1999.

BUNDLES OF JOY
only from

▼ Silhouette®

Available wherever Silhouette books are sold.

If you enjoyed what you just read,
then we've got an offer you can't resist!

Take 2 bestselling love stories FREE!

Plus get a FREE surprise gift!

**Available from May 1999 from
Silhouette Books...**

World's Most
Eligible Bachelors

WYOMING WRANGLER
by Victoria Pade

A RANCHING FAMILY

The whole town was whispering about
Shane McDermot's engagement. Seemingly the
millionaire rancher had set his sights on Maya Wilson,
a woman born out of Elk Creek's most shocking affair.
Were his motives pure...or did more than passion
prompt his proposal?

**Each month, Silhouette Books brings you an
irresistible bachelor in these all-new, original
stories. Find out how the sexiest, most-sought-after
men are finally caught.**

Available at your favorite retail outlet.

Silhouette®

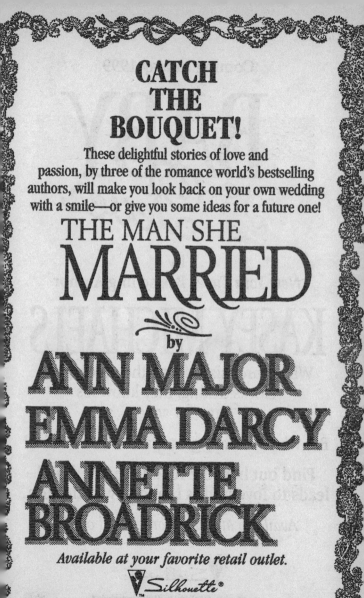

CATCH THE BOUQUET!

These delightful stories of love and passion, by three of the romance world's bestselling authors, will make you look back on your own wedding with a smile—or give you some ideas for a future one!

THE MAN SHE MARRIED

by

ANN MAJOR

EMMA DARCY

ANNETTE BROADRICK

Available at your favorite retail outlet.

Silhouette®

Look us up on-line at: http://www.romance.net

PSBR599

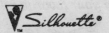

Coming in June 1999 from

Silhouette® Books...

Those matchmaking folks at Gulliver's Travels are at
it again—and look who they're working their magic
on this time, in

HOLIDAY Honeymoons

Two Tickets to Paradise

For the first time anywhere, enjoy these two new
complete stories in one sizzling volume!

HIS FIRST FATHER'S DAY   Merline Lovelace
A little girl's search for her father leads her to
Tony Peretti's front door...and leads *Tony* into the
arms of his long-lost love—the child's mother!

MARRIED ON THE FOURTH   Carole Buck
Can summer love turn into the real thing? When
it comes to Maddy Malone and Evan Blake's
Independence Day romance, the answer is a
definite "yes!"

Don't miss this brand-new release—
HOLIDAY HONEYMOONS: Two Tickets to Paradise—
coming June 1999, only from Silhouette Books.

Available at your favorite retail outlet.

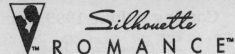

Silhouette ROMANCE™

COMING NEXT MONTH

#1372 I MARRIED THE BOSS!—Laura Anthony
Loving the Boss

Sophia Shepherd wanted to marry the ideal man, and her new boss, Rex Michael Barrington III, was as dreamy as they came! But when an overheard conversation had him testing her feelings, Sophia had to prove she wanted more than just a dream....

#1373 HIS TEN-YEAR-OLD SECRET—Donna Clayton
Fabulous Fathers

Ten years of longing were over. Tess Galloway had returned to claim the child she'd thought lost to her forever. But Dylan Minster, her daughter's father and the only man she'd ever loved, would not let Tess have her way without a fight, and without her heart!

#1374 THE RANCHER AND THE HEIRESS—Susan Meier
Texas Family Ties

City girl Alexis MacFarland wasn't thrilled about spending a year on a ranch—even if it meant she'd inherit half of it! But one look at ranch owner Caleb Wright proved it wouldn't be *that* bad, *if* she could convince him she'd be his cowgirl for good.

#1375 THE MARRIAGE STAMPEDE—Julianna Morris
Wranglers & Lace

Wrangler Merrie Foster and stockbroker Logan Kincaid were *nothing* alike. She wanted kids and country life, and he wanted wealth and the city. But when they ended up in a mock engagement, would the sparks between them overcome their differences?

#1376 A BRIDE IN WAITING—Sally Carleen
On the Way to a Wedding

Stand in for a missing bride? Sara Martin didn't mind, especially as a favor for Dr. Lucas Daniels. But when her life became filled with wedding plans and stolen kisses, Sara knew she wanted to change from stand-in bride to wife forever!

#1377 HUSBAND FOUND—Martha Shields
Family Matters

Single mother Emma Lockwood needed a job...and R. D. Johnson was offering one. Trouble was, Rafe was Emma's long-lost husband—and he didn't recognize her! Could she help him recover his memory—and the love they once shared?